# Deflection!

# Deflection!

Bill Swan

James Lorimer & Company Ltd., Publishers
Toronto

© 2004 Bill Swan

James Lorimer & Company Ltd. acknowledges the support of the Ontario Arts Council. We acknowledge the support of the Government of Canada through the Book Publishing Industry Development Program (BPIDP) for our publishing activities. We acknowledge the support of the Canada Council for the Arts for our publishing program. We acknowledge the support of the Government of Ontario through the Ontario Media Development Corporation's Ontario Book Initiative.

Cover illustration: Greg Ruhl

The Canada Council | Le Conseil des Arts
for the Arts | du Canada

ONTARIO ARTS COUNCIL
CONSEIL DES ARTS DE L'ONTARIO

**National Library of Canada Cataloguing in Publication**

Swan, Bill, 1939–
    Deflection! / written by Bill Swan.

(Sports stories ; 71)
ISBN 1-55028-853-9 (bound).    ISBN 1-55028-852-0 (pbk.)

I. Title. II. Series: Sports stories (Toronto, Ont.); 71.

PS8587.W338D43 2004        jC813'.54        C2004-904822-8

| | |
|---|---|
| James Lorimer & Company Ltd., Publishers<br>35 Britain Street<br>Toronto, Ontario<br>M5A 1R7<br>www.lorimer.ca | Distributed in the United States by:<br>Orca Book Publishers<br>P.O. Box 468<br>Custer, WA USA<br>98240-0468 |

Printed and bound in Canada.

# Contents

*In memory of my father*
*Hap Swan,*
*who drove us to practices*
*on those cold Saturday mornings*
*so long ago;*
*and my cousin*
*Ron Henderson,*
*who invented Grandpa Socks.*

# 1

# The Bear Claws

The day my hockey team got some idea we weren't the worst team ever, Grandpa Gord drove me to the arena. Grandpa Gord is one of my three grandfathers.

We got to the rink at three-thirty, half an hour before game time. It was two weeks before Christmas.

My name is Jake Henry. My team is the Bear Claws. We play in the Oshawa Lakeridge League, which is made up of teams from Oshawa and Clarington. Since it's house league, we're not superstars or anything. Not like some teams you read about in certain books, who travel all over the country and solve murders between tournament games. As if.

In the dressing room I put my stick in the rack. I dumped my equipment out on the floor and started to dress: pants, shin pads, socks. (I had put my jock on at home because there were girls in the dressing room.)

Just as I put my shoulder pads over my head I looked over at Victoria Eldridge, who was struggling with her sweater. Victoria and I take turns at playing goal for the Bear Claws. Victoria glanced over at me with this face she does sometimes that I can't describe.

"What on earth are you doing?" she said, loudly, separating the words the way adults sometimes do. Everybody in the dressing room turned to me.

I could have asked the same question.

"Where are your goal pads?" I asked.

"No, no, no," she said, shaking her head. "It's your turn to play goal, Jake."

Every game Victoria and I alternate playing goal and left defence. We share the goalie equipment, too, since it belongs to the team. Whoever is to play goal the next game is supposed to take the equipment home and bring it to the game.

"We got a problem here?" said Rajah Singh, our coach. Rajah is a good guy, about my Dad's age, with short black hair, a dark complexion, and a moustache with streaks of white in it.

"Jake forgot the goalie stuff," said Victoria, pulling her sweater down and shaking out her hair. It was light brown and came to her shoulders. It frizzed out all over the place with static.

"It's her turn," I replied. "Isn't it? I played last game ..." Oops. That's when I remembered. I hadn't played last game. That game had been cancelled.

Coach Rajah looked at his watch. "We have twenty-one minutes," he said. "Where's your equipment?"

"At home," I said, trying to remember if I was right. If it was my turn to play, the equipment should have been at home.

"Who's here who can get it?"

"Fred's out there," I said. Fred is my stepfather. My mother and father had divorced when I was about three, when I was too young to remember.

"And your Grandpa Cowbells!" said Simon Lee, referring to the odd clanking of bells we could hear even in the dressing room. Simon was a big kid who played defence. He had a space in his upper teeth where a tooth used to be.

Grandpa Gord — or Grandpa Cowbells — is my mother's father. He comes to all my games and brings two cowbells that he rings every time our team scores. Sometimes he gets mixed up and rings the bells when the other team scores. He often does this because he knows squat about hockey. He also is teaching me how to play the violin. Or as he says, to play the fiddle, which he says is different than the violin.

"Go get Fred and see what he can do," said Coach Rajah.

I had just put on my hockey pants and had rolled one stocking over my right shin pad.

"Lemme …" I said.

"Now," said the coach. "Use some of your speed. We don't have all day." Rajah is easygoing, but when he speaks like that, everybody pays attention. And I mean everybody. Including all the parents who like to think they're needed in the dressing room. Yeah. Like a bad itch.

I jammed my foot into one boot, fumbled with the other before giving up. I limped out of the dressing room on one booted foot, shoulder pads crooked, and one shin pad flopping.

In the corridor between the dressing rooms and the boards of the rink, I looked up into the stands. There were another couple of teams on the ice finishing the third period of their game. Somebody hit the boards behind me and the glass rattled my helmet. Up in the stands, Fred was talking to some other parents and Grandpa Gord. I waved my arms until I got his attention. He came over and leaned over the railing.

My stepfather is average size with an average build. He has one blue eye and one brown eye. He teaches at a teachers' college. If you ask him, he'll tell you that he teaches the teachers to teach. If you encourage him at all he will recite a poem about a tutor who taught two kids to toot a flute. I try not to ask him.

"My goalie pads," I yelled. "They're at home."

"Thought you said it was Victoria's turn in net."

"It is, but she and the coach don't agree. The stuff should be there."

"You sure?" he said. "I don't remember seeing them."

"They've gotta be," I said. "Can you go get them? Please? Fast?"

Fred looked down at me with friendly eyes and burst into a slow-motion routine. He reached in his pocket and pulled out his cellphone.

"Good job your mother decided to stay home with Nanny Joyce today to finish her quilt," he said. "If it's there, she could run it over." I could barely hear him over the noise of the game on the ice behind me.

We live a four-minute drive from the new arena on Pebble-stone Road in Courtice. If she made it in five minutes, that would give me fifteen to strap on my pads and stuff. With help we could make it.

Fred put the cellphone to his ear. He looked like he was talking to a playing card. Grandpa Gord kept coming over and repeating, "I'll go, I'll go. If Lisa doesn't answer I'll go and get 'em."

"Where did you say you put your equipment?" Fred yelled, looking down at me. With the other game on the ice behind me, it was not easy to hear.

"In the furnace room, same as always," I said. "On the clothes rack." Fred had built a homemade clothes rack out of dowels and two-by-fours for me to hang my hockey stuff on to dry.

"Not there," Fred said. "Think some more."

I pounded the heel of my hand on my forehead. The time clock showed the game had nine minutes left. The Zamboni would take ten minutes to clear and flood the ice. We had nineteen minutes until ice time. Did I forget to hang the stuff up? I remembered gathering my regular equipment — for playing defence — but didn't have the goalie equipment.

I returned to the dressing room, limping in that one boot. The look in the coach's eyes was something I never want to see again.

"Not at my place," I said, shaking my head. "You sure you don't have the stuff at home?" I asked Victoria. She made face number two, which is even worse than the other face I couldn't describe.

"Sixteen minutes," said Coach Rajah. "Sixteen and counting."

Everyone in the dressing room sat back and went limp. It was as though the whole team was inflatable and somebody had let the air out of us. Except for the coach. You could tell by his colour he was just getting pumped up.

"Well, I ..." I said.

A big, booming voice in the corridor drowned me out.

"Take care, take care, take care."

A huge man bullied his way through the dressing room doorway. Dressed in a blue-and-white nylon jacket, he had salt-and-pepper hair, a white moustache that had never been trimmed, and a grumpy scowl. He carried a big equipment bag on his shoulders, held in place with his left wrist which was bent back to grab the handle. In his other hand he held a goalie stick.

"Stand aside everybody," he said as he came in the room, "I have big feet."

"Grandpa P.J.!" cried Victoria.

Grandpa P.J. was Fred's father. Which made him my step-grandfather. Only I call him Grandpa P.J. Everyone else on the team called him P.J., which he'll tell you stands for Pretty Jolly, but really stands for Peter James. Grandpa P.J. still plays goal himself in two recreation leagues and a Golden Oldsters tournament.

"Somebody forget some equipment?"

Grandpa P.J. threw the goalie stick on the rack where it bounced off and fell to the floor. He brushed by three parents, knocking one against the wall. He spun around to apologize and pushed two others off balance with the equipment bag.

"Excuse me, excuse me, excuse me," he said, dropping the equipment bag, *ker-thunk*, at my feet. "Forgot, didn't you?"

*Now* I remembered. Grandpa P.J. had taken me to our last game in Newtonville. And since I was to play goal the next game, he had put the equipment in the back of his van. But I had gone to a movie with my Dad after the game. I had forgotten the equipment.

I looked up. I mean way up. Grandpa P.J. was at least six foot two — and about the same around the middle. P.J. is one of the reasons I play goal. When my mother married Fred, P.J. took me to see the Oshawa Generals play. He bought me street hockey goal pads, a net, a goalie stick, and would spend hours drilling shots at me in the driveway. He even took me to see him play. How could I not play goal?

"Thanks, P.J." I said, happy, but feeling foolish.

P.J. stood there looking at me for the longest time.

"Well, it's not my fault," I said.

"Don't try to deflect the blame," P.J. said. "You're the goalie. I'm just the dumb guy who drives the van."

Just then Coach Rajah clapped his hands. "Okay," he said. "Let's get with it. We're playing the Cougars remember. They're at the top of the league. Last time they swamped us 9–0 It's time we got a little revenge."

# 2

# Empty Net

By the end of the first period, the Cougars were up on us, 2–1. The second goal had come from a scramble in front of the net. I'd kicked out a shot from their best centre, Lars Allrick.

Lars was a big guy with strength, speed, stick-handling, and a hard shot. He was one of two players on the Cougars who had played rep hockey — that is, the city All-Star team that plays against teams from other cities. Last game he had scored four goals.

Even though I had stopped Lars, our defence let the rebound sit on the ice about four feet in front of me for half an hour.

The Cougars pounced. Two, three of their guys slapped at it. I took one in the belly pad but couldn't hold it. In the scramble I went down to block a low sweep shot. I stopped it but lost sight of the puck.

Players pushed and shoved in the crease. Somebody fell over me. Next thing I knew the puck was in the net behind me.

I had skated to the bench to adjust straps. "The team'll get it back. Don't sweat it," said Rajah.

Sure, I thought. Our guys had slowed down already. I was beginning to fear what might happen in the third period.

One player for the Cougars, Jamie Reisberry, knew me from school. He's a year older than me. He was also the other player on the Cougars who had played rep. Lars had been hurt the year before and his parents had yanked him off the rep team. Reisberry had been a fourth-line player. His parents got tired of travelling every weekend to watch him sit on the bench. Everybody said they should still be playing rep hockey.

Reisberry was also a bully. Once, when I was in kindergarten, he had rubbed rotten apples in my hair on the way home from school. He knew that Grandpa Gord taught me fiddle lessons. He must have shared that with his teammates. They started calling me "Hee-Haw!" Now, for some reason, they also latched onto Willie Westewicz. As I said, Willie isn't the fastest skater in the world. But he is dependable. And strong. He plays road hockey with Victoria and me. He usually won't use his strength — not to body check, anyway. Reisberry and his teammates started calling Willie "Eeyore."

Halfway through the period, with the score still 2–1, Willie fanned on a slap shot. Harvey Hyndman, the Cougars' best defenceman, poked the puck free and rushed by him.

He had five strides on everybody, and our forwards had been deep in the Cougars' zone. There was no chance anybody would catch him. He came in on a breakaway like a freight train. Every goalie's second-worse nightmare.

I stood my ground, gliding high in the crease to cut down the angle, but not so far out I couldn't cover the angles. He wasn't going to deke me. He would have to beat me with a shot.

Harvey tried the deke anyway, shifting to his right and flipping a backhand shot high on my glove side.

I read the move perfectly, hitching up my shoulder to block the shot. The puck bounced straight up and disappeared. Shouts and groans came from the stands and the bench. Something hit my back. I turned just in time to see the puck trickle over the goal line.

*That's* every goalie's worst nightmare.

The razzing from the Cougars' bench got worse after that. What with a Hee-Haw for me and an Eeyore for Willie, soon their bench was snorting with noises like the braying of jack-asses.

"Hee-haw! Hee-haw!"

Rajah would have shut us up pretty fast if we tried anything like that. Their coach didn't seem to mind.

The Cougars kept it up, getting noisier and noisier. Our team began to look like inner tubes with a lot of the air let out.

Near the end of the period, Lars wound up again from their end. He skated around our forwards as though he were dancing. At centre ice, he shifted around Sandie Demeter. She turned to try to keep up with him, but by the time she turned he was over the red line. Willie had been covering the point on left defence. He tried to skate backward to keep between Lars and the goal.

It was a nice try, but Lars was too fast. Willie reached out with his stick to play the puck. Lars turned him inside out and cut to the inside. From the top of the faceoff circle he wound up and let go a slapshot that I never even saw.

4–1.

When the buzzer sounded to end the period, I was relieved. But we still had one full period to play. Our team was already tired, like our legs had fallen off. The third period promised to be shooting practice for the Cougars — with me as target.

At the bench between periods, Coach Rajah turned to Willie. "Use the body," he said. "Use your strength — you're a big guy. Get in front of these clowns, slow them down."

At practices, Rajah always made the team do both defensive and offensive drills. He made us repeat shifting from side to side, following the play, but keeping position. We also practiced bodychecking, which is new to us this year. We all tried our best, but Willie just couldn't get his full weight into it.

Tyler scoffed.

"Yeah, right, Coach. Like that's going to happen. Willie's afraid to bodycheck." Rajah looked at him as though it was none of his business.

The game had become a chore. That is, until halfway through the third. With the Cougars still up by three, David Wrigley split the Cougars' defence and waltzed in on their goalie. I'd like to say he scored. But he rang one off the goalpost. The solid *ping!* echoed through the rink.

Until then, the Cougars had been chanting their donkey bray more and more. David's shot told them the Bear Claws weren't dead yet. It told *us* we weren't done.

Three minutes later Willie quieted the braying completely. He was just over the red line and three Cougars were coming in on him. Just to get rid of the puck he dumped it into their end with a high flip-in.

The puck went over the heads of the Cougars' defence, end over end, as though in slow motion.

It came down about six feet out in front of the Cougars' goal, still bouncing. Now, any goalie will tell you that a bouncing puck is tough — you don't know where it's going.

The Cougars' goalie didn't.

He came out just to take the puck as though he were going to pass it up the side to his defence. But the puck hopped once over his stick. Turning quickly to get it back, he slipped. He reached back with his stick — and knocked the puck into his own net.

The Cougars didn't bray much about that one.

Our bench broke out in the chant: "Ee-yore! Ee-yore! Ee-yore!" before Coach Rajah raised his hand to silence it. But the message had been delivered: 4–2.

I'm not saying that there is a magic answer. The Cougars, especially Lars, Reisberry, and a couple of others, were faster than us. But in that third period we found that if we skated hard, back-checking, then these superstars would have to rush their shots and wouldn't get a second chance.

Supposing, of course, that I stopped the first.

With about three minutes to go, Carl Biro cut in on a rush down the right boards and got a really good shot at the Cougars' net. The goalie stopped it. But Jenny Lau had rushed down her wing and was standing on the edge of the crease. The rebound dropped at her feet. She scored on an easy tap-in.

4–3.

With about forty seconds to go, the play had gone down to the Cougar's end. Coach Rajah signalled to me from the bench.

4–3!

Pull the goalie!

Anyone who knows hockey knows this play. If you're down by one in the last minute of play, you pull your goaltender and send out an extra forward. If you keep the puck in their end, you have an extra player and more chance to score.

Of course, if the other team gets the puck, they can easily score in the empty net. So the risk is only whether you lose by one goal or two.

I raced to the bench, flat out.

I was five feet from the bench when Tyler jumped on the ice and headed for the attack — a sixth skater.

It was a thrill. But sitting on the bench, all I could see was that empty net.

On the attack, Willie got the puck behind the Cougars' net. He centred a pass. Nobody on our team could reach it. Next thing I saw, Reisberry, the Cougar centre, grabbed the puck just inside his own blue line and let go a wrist shot.

The puck rose, floated over centre ice, fell to the ice with a slap at our blue line, and slid wobbling down the ice.

Into our goal.

5–3.

So much for revenge.

In the dressing room later, Coach Rajah held up his hands for attention.

"A good game, everybody," he said. "What I saw out there today, you have applied what we've been practicing."

"We still lost," said Todd.

"And those guys still skated through us like we were soft butter," said Josef Peleg. "Half those guys should be playing rep."

"But they're not," said the coach. "You have something they don't: You are a team. Next game, these guys will be toast."

"Yeah, we did do better this time," said Jenny.

"Tyler bounced one off the crossbar right at the end," said Willie.

"And Willie rang the post in the first period," David Wrigley said.

"Count up the goalposts! We coulda beat them!" said Simon Lee, grinning through his missing tooth. "We coulda!"

"They sure know they were in a hockey game," said Rajah. "That's quite a jump from the 9–0 thumping they gave us in October."

Everyone sat grinning for a moment while that sank in.

"One more thing." Rajah held up his hand, but he already had our attention. "The Backler Tournament. That's three days long right after Christmas. You've all signed, and we've got the fees paid. December 28, 29, 30."

"All right!" several said.

I slumped back on the bench. The Backler Tournament is the most boring tournament in the world. We stay at home. All my relatives would be there. Last year we won the consolation trophy. What I really hoped would happen is the team would go in one of the big tournaments. Any tournament where we would stay in a motel, eat fast food, watch movies, and fizz pop over everything on the bus when we won. Or go to Quebec, where we could sign autographs and solve murders.

"What's the dates again?" asked Victoria.

"December 28, 29, 30. I'll repeat it when the parents get here. And ..."

His voice rose on that last word, and we knew something special was coming. Coach Rajah now had our attention.

"The Cougars are registered, too. Do you guys think it's time for payback?"

When the parents and grandparents and everyone were allowed into the dressing room, we were still yelling and screaming. Coach does know how to get us steamed up, even after a game.

# 3

# Fiddle Faddle

Four days later we were playing road hockey on the street in front of Victoria's house.

"Jacob! Jacob Henry! Time for your fiddle lesson!"

I tried to ignore my mother's voice. She was two doors down, calling from the front door. The game was in front of Victoria's house because she was playing goal. Grandpa Gord's car was in our driveway. I hadn't seen him pull in.

"Shoot it! Shoot it!" yelled Willie.

Victoria moved toward me to cut down the angle. Her street hockey pads were tattered, and a bit ragged. Here it was, ten days before Christmas. She had goalie pads at the top of her Christmas list. Her goalie mask she had painted and re-painted maybe a hundred times, and she was proud of how ugly it looked.

"Intimidation," she would say.

I pulled my stick back for a slapshot. Shmack! The tennis ball was a dirty yellow blur, beating Victoria flat out. But it missed the edge of the goal.

"Almost off the post!" I yelled.

"By a mile!" said Victoria. "Now go chase the ball."

"Can't. Got to go," I said with a smirk, jerking my head back toward my house, where my mother still stood in the front doorway. "Music lesson."

Willie made a face. "If you call that music." He picked up his stick and strummed it like a guitar. "Look at Jake, he's a real farm boy!"

"I'll farm boy you," I said. I held my hockey stick in both hands and gave him a push, sort of a gentle cross-check.

"Hey! Take it easy," Willie replied.

One thing that makes me angry is someone teasing me about Grandpa Gord's music. But especially Willie, after the teasing we went through with the Cougars.

Okay, so Grandpa Gord's music does suck. He plays old-time fiddle music, the kind that might have been okay in a barn dance at a corn husking bee a hundred and fifty years ago.

"The ball?" said Victoria, tipping her mask back.

Victoria is eleven, almost twelve. She has long brown hair and goaltender eyes that won't blink. In street hockey, as with the Bear Claws, we take turns playing goal.

"Don't be such a pig," she said. "Just get the ball."

Six doors down, the dirty yellow ball rolled on, bouncing over the curb, up Mr. Valentine's driveway. It came to rest on the brown grass on his front lawn.

"Get it quick before old man Valentine grabs it," Victoria said. If Mr. Valentine saw the ball first he would keep it. He must have a hundred or more tennis balls stored in his yard.

"Willie can use the skating practice," I said.

Which was true. Willie was bigger and stronger than me, but he couldn't skate as fast. Since we played road hockey in Rollerblades, we got extra skating practice. Though it was December, we had no snow. This was unusual, but sure helped for road hockey.

"Snigglharfamaggotbarf," said Willie. But he skated down the street to get the ball.

Victoria leaned on her goalie stick as we watched him skate down the street.

"Rajah says the Clippers' coach will be at the Christmas tourney," she said, tipping her mask back.

"You mean the girls' rep team?" I asked.

"That's them. I really want to try out for them next year. Coach Rajah says they're looking for a goalie for next year, too."

I didn't quite know what to say. Rep hockey? I'd die for a chance to play rep hockey, but I would never tell anybody that. I mean, right away they would start thinking you saw yourself as a superstar. Victoria had never mentioned this before.

"Wow!" I said, "next you'll be wanting to go to the Olympics."

Victoria gave me a fierce look.

"Oh, I do," she said. "And thanks for the vote of confidence, jerk."

She pulled her mask back down as Willie came up the street without the tennis ball. Mr. Valentine had scored again.

"We'll put the net in your garage when we're done," Victoria yelled after me as I skated home. "Twit."

My mother had gone inside by the time I got to the front door. Inside, Grandpa Gord played a jig. Grandma Joyce accompanied him at a portable keyboard.

"Ta-teedle-deedle-deedle da-da teedle-deedle-da, ta teedle-deedle ..."

Since my friends weren't watching, the music made me want to tap my feet. This is difficult in Rollerblades.

"Get those things off in the house!" said my mother in the firm voice she uses for rattling dishes. She spoke louder than usual to be heard over the music. I rolled along the tiles in the front hall. I opened the garage door to put my hockey stick away.

"And don't just throw that in there," she added. "Honestly, you're as bad as Fred."

Mom was doing four things at once. She had dinner started. I could smell the shepherd's pie in the oven. The central vacuum hose lay under the dining room table. In her hand she had a quilt patch with a needle sticking out of it. She would go downstairs and do something with it. About two months later she would show off a finished quilt.

I tossed my hockey stick into the garage. It landed on the old rocking chair that was stacked on top of the old-fashioned pine box where we stored the artificial Christmas tree.

"Honestly, that man …" my mother continued, shaking her head. She was still dressed in her jogging outfit. She runs five miles every day.

Fred came up from his office den in the lower level with an empty coffee cup in his hand.

"Here is that man," he said, smiling. "Just in time for whatever it is. What is it?"

"The garage," said Grandpa Gord.

Fred smiled. "So the garage is messy. I'm not a neat freak." He began reciting, "A teacher who teaches teachers to teach, tried to …"

"I've heard it, Fred," I said. Fred's okay, but he has this way of repeating stuff nobody wants to hear. Teachers are like that.

"Your fiddle's on the table," said Grandpa Gord. Grandpa Gord and Nanny Joyce are my mother's parents. Ever since before I started school, Grandpa Gord has been trying to teach me how to play the fiddle. He always dresses in western cowboy shirts with fancy frills across the chest, blue denim jackets with fancy sewing on them, and a big cowboy hat from the Calgary Stampede. And cowboy boots.

I could play some tunes. He was now trying to teach me stuff with half notes, quarter notes, eighth notes, and worse. It was tough keeping time, and I couldn't play the eighth notes and stuff like that without botching up the timing altogether. Besides, who do you know wants to listen to old-time fiddle music? It's not what you boast about to your friends. Guess what, teammates? I can now play "Turkey in the Straw."

You can imagine how that would make my team dance in the dressing room.

Now Sting, or even AC/DC, maybe Rush. Those were bands that my dad listened to when he was a teen. Still listens to.

Grandpa Gord put some rosin on his bow, and positioned his fiddle under his chin.

"Try it this way," he said. "Keep the bow steady and make your fingers do the work." He had a voice full of gravel and a face to match.

We were working on a jig. Every time I got to the part with the trilly little notes, I tried to get my fingers to move fast, from one string to the other. When I did that, I forgot to bow and everything came up clunkers.

"No, no, no," Grandpa Gord said. "Remember, the strings do all the work, so you have to control them. But the sound is made by the violin. That little box is shaped just so. The sound deflects off every curvy corner and teams up with other sounds so that what comes out is the rich fiddle sound."

"I can't move my fingers fast enough," I said.

"That's what practice is for. You have been practicing, haven't you?"

"You have a game today?" Fred asked. He has this annoying habit of asking questions when he knows the answer. He does it to remind me I have a hockey game. He really believes he is not nagging when he does it that way. I'd rather he not remind me. Besides, there is no chance I would forget a hockey game or hockey practice. Not in a megamillion years. Fiddle lessons I put up with because it makes Grandpa Gord happy, and sometimes I forget it is practice time. But not hockey. When I was three years old, I kept a make-believe Zamboni in the cupboard under the kitchen sink.

"Four o'clock," I replied, continuing to play along with Grandpa Gord. "Courtice A."

"I'll be there, cowbells on," said Grandpa Gord. He accompanied me in a reel and covered up when I slurred the sixteenth notes. How somebody with fingers all hard and stiff from working on farms and construction could move so fast on those tiny strings I'll never know.

"Hey! And some really good news," Fred said. "Your father just e-mailed me. All your cousins are coming down over the holidays."

"You'd think maybe he'd let *me* know," I said. "Like, duh."

"Yeah, but then you'd check your e-mail the day after New Year's," said Fred. "Besides, he said he did e-mail you. Five days ago. Checked it lately? Anyway, you're gonna have a real family gathering."

My Dad has a sister who lives in Cape Breton, and a brother in Calgary. They have three kids each. These are my cousins, though I don't think I've seen them more than two or three times.

"Haven't seen Yvonne and Dave for ages," said Nanny Joyce. "Since their kids were babies. They must be in school now."

"Wasn't Dave the one who wanted me to play classical violin?" asked Grandpa Gord, with a chuckle. His voice was crimped from holding the violin under his chin.

"When are they coming?" asked my mom.

Fred reached into his pocket and pulled out a folded sheet. "Here, read it," he said. "Just before New Year's, I think. About the 28th, 29th. He just wants to make sure Jake's all set to go down to London for a couple of days to join 'em."

Sometimes I think my family is the most complicated in the world. See, my Dad, who lives in London, was married to my mom. They got divorced when I was three. My mom married Fred. So Grandpa Gord and Nanny Joyce used to be my father's in-laws, and they know all my dad's family. And they all know each other. Unlike a lot of divorced families, they all get along. It's hard to explain to my friends how my father can sit down and have coffee with Fred and my mom like they were old buddies.

"It would have been nice if he'd given you a bit more notice," said my mother. "But that's about what I would expect." She read the message and picked up a green marker to put it on the dry-erase calendar in the kitchen where we mark stuff.

"Uh-oh," she said, standing in front of the calendar.

"What is it?" I asked.

"Your hockey tournament," she said. "That's when your hockey tournament is on."

Grandpa Gord made a small, uh-oh sound on his fiddle, trying to be funny, but I didn't think it was funny at all.

# 4

# Family Fuss

I won't go." I jammed myself down in the seat. We were in a coffee shop. My father had insisted on the meeting.

"It's the first chance in five years you've had to see your cousins," my father repeated for the umpteenth time. "It's not that this happens every year."

My father is a thin man. He has a thin face, thin nose, thin arms. Thin whiskers, which he sometimes grows into a thin beard. Sometimes, like now, even his voice is thin.

"It's that it is happening this year," I replied. "Why can't they just stay in Cape Breton and Saskatchewan …"

"It's Alberta. Calgary is in Alberta."

"Wherever." I crossed my arms, jammed my baseball cap down hard, and tried to look angry. Well, actually, I was, kind of. I was more afraid, really. Afraid that my father would be reasonable, and friendly, and I would end up agreeing with him. I couldn't do that. As if.

My father's name is Dann. Dann Henry. He spells it like that, too, although his given name is Daniel. I saw that on his birth certificate. He's a graphic artist. He does Web sites and newspaper and magazine ads, all from his home in London. That's about three hours from our place in Courtice. To get to my dad's place we have to drive through Toronto on the 401 or spend eight hours on a train each way. Ever since he and my mother got divorced he has lived alone, except every second weekend when I stay at his place.

"Look," he said. He was angry. His voice became deep and though he wasn't shouting, it rattled spoons on the table. "Your aunt and uncle and their kids are coming from Cape Breton. Harold and Lucy and their kids are coming from Alberta. They are all going to be here for three days. In London. It's a chance for everybody to get together with Grandpa Ron."

I shrugged.

"It's family," he said, letting out a sigh that told me I might be winning.

"My family," he added.

In the silence that fell between us, other customers in the coffee shop continued to talk. Someone dropped a tray. Dishes rattled in the kitchen. Silverware clanged and the sounds echoed off hard walls.

"It's my favourite tournament," I said. "I do this every year."

"Once, Jake. You did it once." he replied. "Besides, tournaments come every year. Your family doesn't."

"Oh, yeah," I said. "You want me to go all the way down to London to see boring people I don't even know." I stared at him while he fiddled with his coffee cup. "It's our chance to beat the Cougars," I said, lying. I thought we had as much chance of beating the Cougars as we had of playing rep hockey. Sure.

"You'll meet them again in the playoffs," he said. "And I'm not bargaining with you. This is non-negotiable, son."

"You'd understand if you played hockey."

My dad has never played hockey. Even his father, Grandpa Ron, still plays. Fred still plays once a week; even Grandpa P.J. plays in about six leagues, but that was because he plays goal.

It's not that you have to skate hard or anything. Pickup teams everywhere always need goalies.

"Whether I played hockey or not makes no difference," he said. "That's a red herring. This is about Christmas. And family."

"Family?" I said. "I'm getting sick of family. You'd think they'd give a guy a little room."

I started to gather my stuff up. I knocked a coffee cup on the floor. "If this is all about Christmas, then let's keep it at Christmas, okay? Let them come on Christmas, and Grandpa Ron can take me to London and see them all. Or," I brightened as though I'd just thought of it, "Or on New Year's. That'd be good. We could all go skating. Isn't that what they did in the old days, go skating and stuff on outdoor ponds? So how about they fit their visit around what I want to do?"

I headed for the door.

"I can't believe we're having this talk," my father said, mainly to himself as he picked up the coffee cup and a napkin. "Three days before Christmas."

* * *

Late on the afternoon of Christmas Eve, Grandpa Ron pulled into our driveway. Willie and I were playing hockey. Victoria had gone home.

Grandpa Ron, as I said, is my father's father. Well, I thought, no way is he going to talk me into giving up my hockey tournament.

Every Christmas Eve, Mom and Fred invite everybody for dinner. Grandpa Ron, my dad, Grandpa P.J., Grandpa Gord, and Nanny. They did it to show how good they all got along. As usual, my dad couldn't make it.

"So, Dann tells me you're not going to London next week,"

Grandpa Ron said, walking over to where we were playing. "We're going to miss you."

"Dad threatened to kidnap me," I said, not nicely. "But I won't go. I have a hockey tournament." I tried to look firm. All this family stuff — a guy has to put his foot down.

"Hockey tournament," I repeated, and Grandpa Ron nodded.

I turned and lifted my hockey stick. I slapped a shot toward the hockey goal in the middle of the street, where Willie stood waiting to play. Willie ducked. The tennis ball bounced off the shaft of his stick and into the top corner of the net. It stuck in the mesh.

"Your dad doesn't understand," Grandpa Ron added. "He never did play hockey."

No one spoke for a moment. Sometimes I'm not sure when Grandpa Ron is pulling my leg.

"That slapshot is so wild," he said, "that you need somebody to stand by the net with a scoop shovel to deflect it in."

Willie looked at him. "What's a scoop shovel?" he asked.

Grandpa Ron ignored the question. He kicked the tennis ball back to me.

"Bet you can't do it again. That tip-in shot."

I grinned. Not likely. Then I saw he was still serious.

"No, really," he said. "Try it again." I shrugged. Willie grinned. "See, that's the problem with your slapshot. You never know where it's going. Now, in my day, our coach had us practicing a good solid wrist shot. Accuracy, that's what counts."

He held out a hand and borrowed my stick.

"Something like this," he said, feathering the ball with the tip of the stick. "It's all in the wrist."

He took a shot from about eight feet in front of the goal. It missed the far post by another eight feet.

"Well, a little rusty. But you get the idea." He handed me back my stick.

He turned to Willie. "I ever tell you I went to high school with Bobby Hull?" He had told Willie three dozen times. Maybe more.

Without waiting for an answer, he added: "Bobby Hull. Brent Hull's father. Played Junior B with the Woodstock Athletics, back in '54–'55. Won the Ontario championship. The year before he went to St. Kitts."

"Brett. It's Brett Hull."

"I said Brent Hull, didn't I? So, okay, work on that wrist shot. And don't worry about next week. It's a three-day tourney, right? If it happens you get beat out on the second day or something, give us a call, we'll find a way to get you down. But I understand. I'd a done the same thing myself. When I was your age."

He gave me a playful poke on the shoulder. "See you at dinner," he said. "And remember, wrist shot, okay?"

When he left, Willie screwed up his face and did that funny thing with his eyes, but he didn't say anything.

# 5

## Consolation Round

For Christmas, Victoria's grandparents gave her new goalie pads, gloves, helmet, shoulder pads — the works.

"Wow! That must have cost a bundle," said Willie, when she told us. We were playing street hockey on Boxing Day. There was still no snow. Victoria was wearing the tattered old street pads. But she wanted to show the new stuff off.

"Come on in," she said. "You really gotta see this. Like, wow."

At her house, we took off our shoes at the side door. Willie was embarrassed because he had holes in his socks.

"Have a look at this!"

Her new goalie stuff was spread out around the Christmas tree. Other presents were pushed back under the tree. Victoria had a sister who was about six. Even her doll carriage was pushed behind the tree, almost out of sight.

We crept into the living room. Victoria picked up one of the red and blue goalie pads and handed it to me.

"How do you like that?" she said. "Aren't they great?"

"Sure are," I replied. I held the pad over my shin and pounded with a fist. "Can't even feel that," I said. "You won't even feel slap shots with these."

Victoria's mother came in from the kitchen. She was drying

a coffee mug. "You guys finished outside?" Mrs. Eldridge had always called Victoria and Willie and me "guys" — as though she had wished that Victoria had been a boy. Victoria didn't seem to mind. Although there was no doubt about her being a girl. All the guys at school thought she looked hot. That is, until they had to play hockey against her. An elbow in the snout will change your mind about a lot of things.

"Vickie's grandparents went really overboard this time," she said. Mrs. Eldridge had blondish hair. She still wore her jogging suit. We had seen her out running earlier with my mom.

"Now we won't have to share the team's goalie equipment," I said. "Be handy."

"Oh, even more than that," said Mrs. Eldridge. "We're going to talk to Coach Rajah about Vickie playing goal every game. She will be trying out for the girls' rep team next year. You all move up an age group. I had doubts enough about her playing full contact this year. You guys are all getting pretty big and fast. But she needs all the ice time she can get."

"But I …"

"Don't you worry about it," said Mrs. Eldridge, returning to the kitchen. "We'll do all the arranging with the coach. And this will allow you to concentrate on your skating. Now you guys run along and play."

"But I …" I knew I was repeating myself.

"Come on, let's go," said Willie, steering me by the elbow.

At the side door we jammed our shoes on. I didn't say anything. Once we got outside, though, I turned to Vickie.

"You didn't say anything about playing goal all the time!" I said. I was angry.

"I … I was going to talk to you about it," she said. "Mostly it was Mom's idea. After Na and Gramps spent all that on the goalie equipment. They all thought then I should be a full-time goalie."

"And you?" I snarled. "Did you bother to mention that I played goal, too? Or did that occur to anybody?"

"I said I was sorry," Vickie said.

"No you didn't!" I snapped. "And you aren't. We'll see what Coach says about it!"

Willie picked up his stick and ragged the tennis ball down the street. We had left the goal in the middle of the street. Someone had moved it to one side. Willie moved it back into the street and flipped a few shots into the net. Victoria and I kind of glared at each other.

Finally, Willie said: "Is it really true what your mother said?" he asked, looking at Victoria. "About trying out for the rep team next year?"

She didn't answer. I didn't wait for her to. I picked up the net by the crossbar and carried it home. I didn't feel like playing street hockey anymore that day.

# 6

# Hockey Violence

Coach Rajah looked around the dressing room and sighed. "This all we have?" he said. I counted twelve players. For one thing, Victoria was not there.

"Vickie was supposed to start in goal today," said the coach. He looked at me as though I was supposed to know something about why she wasn't there. "But she has a try-out with the Clippers."

"Hey, that's great!" said Jenny. "She'll make it. She's good."

"Does that mean we'll lose her?" asked Tyler. "We need her."

"So what's Jake, then?" asked Willie. "Chopped liver?"

Today was the third day of the Backler Tournament. We had played four games — two each day. Victoria played goal for the first game, all shiny in her new pads. She must have said something to her parents, and they must have *not* said something to the coach. I played in the second game. The second day we did the same thing: she played goal the first game, I played the second.

Now, here it was the third day. We had won two games. Any other time our team would have been excited. But Victoria and I weren't speaking and everyone else knew it. Willie grunted a little but tried to keep away from both of us so he wouldn't have to take sides.

"Well," said Coach Rajah, lifting his baseball cap by the peak and scratching his head. "We got this far with two wins. This is the consolation final."

We all leaned back when he said that. We all knew at the beginning of the tournament that the finals would be on the third day. What we didn't know at the beginning was whether we would be in the consolation finals or the final finals — the championship finals. With only two wins out of four games, we had known the day before where we stood.

It was Tyler who asked, "Who do we play?"

All eyes came up to the coach. He smiled like he had a secret.

"Your old friends," he said. "The Cougars."

"You're kidding," said Todd. "You gotta be kidding."

"Wish I were," said Rajah. He looked around the room at the empty places. "I knew we were going to be lean on this last day. But there are two or three people who promised to be here."

"We don't stand a chance without all our players," said Josef. A few parents shuffled in and out of the dressing room.

Fred came into the dressing room to tighten the straps on my goal pads.

Grandpa P.J. and Grandpa Ron squeezed into the dressing room behind him. "Remember, keep your stick flat on the ice," said Grandpa P.J. "Watch the five-hole."

"Didn't have no five-hole when I played," said Grandpa Ron. As usual, his pant legs were too short and his socks didn't match. He wore a Leafs toque and a heavy sweater that was buttoned crooked. "Goalies used to learn to keep their pads together."

"Sometimes I wonder where they get these coaches," said Grandpa P.J.

I rolled my eyes. "Grandpa Ron, it's the butterfly," I said.

"We're supposed to stand that way."

Sandie Demeter looked at me strangely.

"Like, how many grandfathers do you have?" she asked.

"Yeah, where's Grandpa Cowbells?" asked Todd. "Or did he get all jingled out at Christmas?"

"He's out there," replied Fred. "With bells on." On cue, we could hear Grandpa Gord's bells, sounding like a lost reindeer.

Grandpa P.J. tweaked my nose. "Keep your chin up," he said. "Straps okay? Here, let me give that a little heft." He reached down and pulled at my straps. One was loose. He gave it a yank and tightened it up one notch.

"There. That'll do. Don't want you tripping over yourself."

I nodded.

"See you on the ice," said Fred.

"You okay?" asked Grandpa Ron.

I shrugged. Christmas had been kind of quiet since the argument with my dad over the tournament.

"I thought you'd be in London," I said to Grandpa Ron.

"Drove down from London this morning," he replied. "Your cousins had a plane to catch. I dropped them off at the airport. Thought I might as well come on here."

He patted the top of my helmet as though he were ruffling my hair. He smiled.

"Kick butt," he said.

On the way out, Grandpa Ron stood by the stick rack for a moment. "Great idea," he said. "Somebody's been thinking. In my day we used to throw the sticks on the floor and trip over them."

Several of my teammates, several parents, and Coach Rajah looked at him strangely, and then looked at me as though he were my fault.

"Back in the village of Bright, Ontario, when I was a kid, the

men's team won the Ontario Rural Hockey Association title,"
Grandpa Ron said to Grandpa P.J. on the way out the door. "That
was '49–'50, something like that …" Grandpa P.J. rolled his eyes
at me and gave me the thumbs up. Grandpa Ron's voice continued
as they went into the corridor. Something about cigarette smoke
and oranges in the dressing room between periods.

\* \* \*

Up in the stands as the game began, Grandpa Gord rang his
cowbells, Grandpa P.J. could be heard bellowing advice, and
Grandpa Ron had one message every time one of our players
tried a slap shot:

"Wrist it! Wrist it!"

I could look up in the stands and see him talking to P.J. or Fred
or my Dad. Without hearing him, I knew what he was saying:

"They never know where that slapshot is going."

Despite being short several players, we didn't do too badly.
The Cougars were short players, too. Two of their best players
didn't show up. Somebody said it was because they played for
two teams and were playing in a tournament in Goderich.
Unfortunately, good old Lars Allrick wasn't one of the missing.
He scored both of the Cougar goals.

By the third period, though, the score was tied, 2–2. With
only a couple of minutes left, Lars picked up a loose puck just
outside of his blue line and came in on me for a breakaway.

I played him just about perfectly — high enough in the
crease to cut down the angle, not too far out to give him room
to deke me.

He faded left, cut back right and let go a quick wrist shot. I
thrust out my blocker on my stick side. The puck bounced off
into the corner.

Lars had turned the other way. I skated out to retrieve the puck and shot it up the right side to where Simon was skating back, hard. Just as I shot the puck to him I felt the *ping* as one of my straps let go. I could feel the pad shifting. My skate caught on a piece of the strap.

Meanwhile, Simon had grabbed the puck and circled to his right. Lars cut up in front of the goal and stole the puck from him. He circled back and shot a lazy lifter of a wrist shot toward the goal, one I likely could have caught with my bare hands, it was that slow.

But I was in no position for snagging anything. I stumbled on the skate strap, spun around in a circle the opposite way, my arms thrashing around as I tried to get my balance. As I fell, I reached out with my stick to swat the puck out of the air.

I did, too. I could hear the *click* as the stick caught the edge of the puck and changed its direction. It wasn't enough. The puck boinged off the post and into the net.

3–2 for the Cougars.

It was what happened next I'll always remember.

As I hit the ice in a belly flop, I felt the stick hit the puck. The knob of the tape on the handle wasn't enough. The stick slipped out of my hand and took off like a big boomerang, spinning end over end in the air.

It caught Lars right in the smile he always wears after scoring a goal, right under his visor and straight into his teeth. He went down like he had been hit with an axe. Sprawled in front of the net, I could see him fling his gloves in both directions and grab his mouth.

Blood ran through his fingers. The whistle blew, and his coach and trainer came over the boards. I wanted to go over and help him, tell him I was sorry, how sick I felt about it.

I didn't get a chance to, and didn't see much more.

Jamie Reisberry and Harvey Hyndman were on top of me before I could get up. Reisberry went down on one knee and began pounding me on the side of my head.

Harvey dragged Reisberry away as the referee arrived. I started to get up and looked him in the eye. He hadn't hurt me. My helmet and mask protected me.

"You just watch yourself, Henry," Reisberry snarled at me, while the referee held him. "We'll get you back. We'll get you back."

Even while the referee pinned his arms, Reisberry struggled as though he would still go at me if he could. Harvey nudged against him, and I thought for a moment he was being decent. Surely he saw that the whole thing had been an accident. As if I would throw a stick to hurt someone on purpose.

But Reisberry stopped struggling, and the referee guided him to his bench. Harvey went with him, but I could see the words he mouthed. He had a hand on Reisberry's shoulder and he looked back at me, his face twisted.

"Later. We'll get him, later."

He gripped his stick in one hand and made a fist. Still looking me right in the eye, he jabbed his fist toward me.

\* \* \*

"I didn't mean it," I told Grandpa P.J. after the game. "My stick just slipped."

"I'm sure that's true," he replied. "But it was your stick. You're supposed to control your stick at all times."

I felt sick about hitting Lars, seeing him lying there and all the blood and stuff. All I got was a two-minute penalty, but that pretty much ended our hopes of even tying the Cougars. Coach Rajah couldn't pull me for an empty-net attack, not one player down. As it was, I let in another weak one and we lost 4–2.

"Well, it's a caution what can happen out there," said Grandpa Gord.

We had all gone to a coffee shop after the game.

"Is Lars going to be okay?" I asked. The more I thought about Lars the worse I felt.

"That's the eleventy-leventh time you've asked that," said Grandpa Gord. "He may have lost a tooth or two."

"Players are covered with insurance," said Fred, who hadn't said much up to now. "Coach Rajah said that would cover the costs."

"That's just what we would all need," said my mother, "is a lawsuit over injuries. That would just ice the cake." She looked at my dad with that look she sometimes gets that says anything that goes wrong is his fault.

"Lars would be better off taking flute lessons," my father replied. "That's for sure."

Grandpa P.J. flicked a couple of drops of coffee from his spoon at me. "Well, what's done is done," he said. "No use crying over lost teeth. If everybody who got hurt playing hockey …"

"What? You don't think hockey injuries count as real injuries?" asked Grandpa Gord. "Tell that to young Lars."

"It's a violent game," said Grandpa P.J. He always wore that blue and white nylon jacket with a grease stain high on the left sleeve. "There's going to be injuries. Ever see my scar?"

He pulled at his left eye. You could see the white streak of a scar right on the soft skin around his eye socket. "Stick caught me in a pond game when I was twelve," he said. "I got home, it was bleeding pretty bad. My mother taped it up with a band-aid. Doctor once told me it should have had three, four stitches. These things happen."

"If you had the stitches," I said, "maybe you wouldn't have the scar. Then what would you show us?"

Grandpa P.J. looked startled. Then he reached out to try that flip thing where he pretends to chuck my chin and then flips me under the nose. He missed, and we both laughed.

"That's all well and good," said Fred. "But next you'll be saying that fighting is good for hockey. These kids just got into body contact this year. Are you saying we should encourage them to fight, too?"

Grandpa P.J.'s eyes twinkled. I never know whether he is serious about some of this stuff.

"Fighting's part of the game," he said. "Take away that in the pros then there'd be a lot more stick swinging. Remember the Russians in the '70s, used to kick with skates?"

"Not if they threw them out for the season for such non-sense," said my mother, who up to now had been awfully quiet. "Get rid of the violence by turfing out those who fight, hit others with sticks, that sort of thing."

Grandpa P.J.'s eyes danced. "Guys like Jake, here, you mean? Mean stick swingers? Is that who you mean? Okay, Jake, you're gone for the season. One more incident and you're banned from hockey for life."

"But that was an accident ..."

"Sure, sure," said Grandpa P.J. "That's what they all say."

Grandpa Gord brushed an imaginary piece of lint off the frills over his shirt pocket and adjusted his cowboy hat.

"Just a pity that there can't be more harmony in the hockey rink," he said. "We don't seem to have any fights at band practice."

"No," said Grandpa P.J. "But when you play at dances the fights are all out in the parking lot."

# 7

## Sour Notes

January and February were the slowest, coldest months of my life. For one thing, it was too cold to play road hockey, if you can imagine that.

For another, Victoria still wasn't speaking to me. Oh, sure, she would still say things like, "Jake, you could have skated faster," or, "I thought you'd have stopped that one." But if I tried to talk to her about rep hockey, she'd turn frosty, like somebody had turned on the air conditioner in winter.

My mom and Vickie's mom hadn't run together all winter. Not even indoors at the Oshawa Civic Track where they both ran in bad weather. Even Fred had mentioned that, but only a couple of times. Mom said that it was nothing, in that way that means it is *something*, but she doesn't want to talk about it. Not in front of me, anyway.

Victoria hadn't made the Clippers team. Not for this year, anyway. She wouldn't even talk about that with Willie — and they were still buds.

I had almost forgotten about the stick incident with Lars, even though we had played the Cougars twice more after Christmas. Lars had lost a tooth and even had his picture in the local paper pretending to be Bobby Clarke.

One Saturday, early in March, Grandpa Gord came over as

usual for my fiddle lesson. He was still trying to get me to get the grace notes, but I just couldn't get it right.

"No, no, no, no," said Grandpa Gord, quietly, shaking his head like something was stuck in it. "You have to make it flow. Those are quarter notes. Like this."

He cradled his fiddle in his left arm. He played the three bars easily, his fingers dancing on the strings.

"I'll work on doing it quicker," I said. The thing about having Grandpa Gord for a teacher is that when you can't do stuff right he feels it's *his* fault.

"It's not a matter of quicker," he said. "It's timing. You have to be able to feel the music, feel the right time. When you do that, your fingers will get it right. Now let's try it eight more times."

That's another thing about Grandpa Gord's music lessons. Other teachers would say, "Let's try that again" — and then make you do it eight more times. Grandpa Gord was honest.

I tried the same three bars eight more times. Each time something was still wrong. On the extra beat I was either too fast or too slow. Then it messed up my timing for the rest of the tune.

"It'll come, Jake," said Grandpa Gord. "Sleep on it a few times and your brain will figure it out."

My mother emerged at the top of the steps from the basement and put a finger to her lips so Grandpa Gord couldn't see. She meant, "Don't argue." Grandpa Gord has a lot of strange ideas and usually you are better off not asking him to explain.

"Next week," Grandpa Gord said. He began putting his fiddle in its case. Lesson over. I took the cue and put mine away, too.

"That quilt rack work okay?" Grandpa Gord asked. He was talking to my mother. Mom and Nanny Joyce were making a quilt. Every time they came over for my music lesson, Mom would take Nanny Joyce to the basement workroom. They would sew and stuff. Grandpa Gord had seen a quilt rack in the craft store and decided he could build one like it better and cheaper.

"A hundred and fifty bucks they wanted," he said. "Can you believe that? For a bit of PVC tubing and eight joint things. Cost me twenty bucks in parts. Ron's coming over to have a look. He may order one, too."

Grandpa Gord had brought the quilt rack over for the first time that afternoon. The thing looked a bit like a street hockey goal without the net.

Grandpa Gord glanced at his watch and started to fidget like it was time to leave.

"How's hockey coming?" he said. "You must be getting near playoffs. Those two guys on the Cougars give you any trouble?"

I was surprised when he mentioned this. He never had before, and I didn't think he even knew what had happened out there in that tournament game after Christmas. Aside from the fact that I lost my stick and it hit Lars.

As it was, a friend of Reisberry's goes to my school. He had come up to me smiling just the week before. "You're gonna get creamed," he said. "Next game, maybe the one after. Jamie and Harvey said they were gonna get you good."

I didn't want to tell Grandpa Gord that. He would want to hang a cowbell on them both. Instead, I said, "Naw, that was a long time ago. And yeah, we have playoffs coming up."

Somebody rapped on our front door.

I knew right away who it was. Anybody else would ring the bell. Anybody but Willie. Somehow, Willie thought that if he knocked on the door with the taped knob of his hockey stick he wouldn't disturb anybody the way ringing the doorbell would.

"Want to come out and play some?" Willie asked. He had his Rollerblades on with his street hockey helmet and hockey gloves.

We hadn't played road hockey since that time before the Christmas tournament. That was partly because of the thing with Victoria over playing goal. But mainly it was the snow and cold. Once the first snowstorm hit, road hockey in Rollerblades just wasn't possible.

"Now?" I asked, like I was stunned.

"No, not now, two weeks from now," Willie replied. "I'll just stand here in my skates and wait until Easter."

Willie could do that — tell you you've said something stupid with sarcasm — but without making you feel you were ... well, stupid.

I found my skates and stuff and joined him on the driveway. Victoria was waiting as well.

"Thought maybe we could get some shots," Willie said.

I pulled my net out of the garage. We parked both the goals on the street. Mr. Valentine drove by, scowling and raising a fist. He rolled a window down a crack and said: "Keep the gull-darned balls off my lawn!" We dragged the net out of his way. He didn't look at us, but kept his black eyes and hawk-like nose pointed straight ahead.

We all did a few shots on net. Then Willie and I tried some one-on-one, with Victoria in goal. Our in-line skates worked well on the dry pavement. The cold winter felt like sandpaper. We all began to shiver.

"Coach Rajah call you yet?" Victoria asked, finally.

Willie was doing some shots on goal, while I parked on the crease for rebounds. Only there were no rebounds. Willie used his slapshot and missed the net each time. That's okay. We made him chase after the ball.

"No," I said, "he hasn't called me. What's up?"

"We play the Cougars in a best of three in the first round," Willie said, as he took off down the street after the twelfth straight shot missed the net.

"Starting Monday," said Victoria.

In January and February we had met the Cougars twice in league games. Both games I had played goal. Harvey and Reisberry kept skating up and giving me little cross-checks. A couple of times Reisberry had slashed at me when the ref wasn't looking. The goalie pads took most of the abuse. The Cougars won both games. In fact, they had beaten us every game all year.

"Man, why did they have to match us with the top team?" asked Willie.

"Because we're the bottom. That's the way it goes: top team against the bottom, second team against the second bottom. You know that." I liked to figure out standings and stats. The pairings didn't surprise me.

"You'll be in goal for the first game," Victoria said.

She said it coolly, still upset. I thought I should be the one upset. I mean, we had agreed at the first of the season about taking turns in goal. She was the one who wanted to change that. Well, her grandparents were. And her parents. Sometimes adults get involved and things turn bad.

Willie seemed to be taking a long time getting the ball. I looked down toward Valentine's. Willie was coming back. Without the ball.

"What happened?" I asked.

"Old man Valentine," Willie replied. "The ball was on his lawn. He wouldn't give it back."

"The old grump," said Victoria.

We use a ball instead of a puck in road hockey because it

moves easier. Victoria reached back to the top of the net and took down one of those orange, hollow pucks. They're too light to shoot right, but they have one advantage: you can take one in the shins and it doesn't hurt.

"Try this," she said.

Willie tried a couple of shots with the puck. It didn't roll as far down the road, so we didn't have to race Mr. Valentine for it. But even with it, Willie couldn't hit the net.

Grandpa P.J. pulled into our driveway. He often turned up on Saturday. "Old Odd Socks here yet?" he said as he got out of the car.

"Is he supposed to be?" I asked. "How come?"

"Your mother's birthday, Einstein," he replied. "It's supposed to be a surprise to her, not you."

To Willie he said: "You learning to use that muscle yet? Throw the old body around, bodycheck?"

Willie didn't answer.

Just then Grandpa Ron drove up. As he got out of the car, Willie let a slapshot go that missed by more than a metre — as usual.

"Can that slapshot," said Grandpa Ron. "You never know where it's going."

"It's good for his skating," said Grandpa P.J. as Willie headed down the street again to get the ball from Mr. Valentine's lawn.

"Kids today," said Grandpa Ron. That day he had one purple sock and one red sock. To Grandpa P.J. he said, "Birthday party start yet?" He turned to Willie. "They never know where that slapshot is going," he said.

"Yeah," replied Grandpa P.J. "I keep telling the girl, keep your stick on the ice. Jake, too, does the same thing. I'm going to go out next practice and help the coach. Some of these kids need extra work on the fundamentals."

He turned to Victoria. "By the way, congratulations," he said. He turned to Grandpa Ron. "She's going to be working out at practice with the Clippers for the rest of the year."

"That the rep team? She leaving the Bear Claws?"

"Ask her."

Grandpa Ron turned to Victoria. "Are you? Leaving the Bear Claws?"

Victoria looked at me and smirked. "Not this season. I'm just practicing with them for now. I'm trying out for next year."

"Give you a leg up trying out for next year," Grandpa P.J. said.

"You didn't tell me," I said, surprised.

"You haven't spoken to me since Christmas," she said. "What did you expect?"

"You getting enough ice time?" Grandpa Ron asked, looking at me. "That happens sometimes in the playoffs," he said, more to Grandpa P.J. than anyone. "Coaches get hungry to win, let some kids sit on the bench."

I don't know where he got that idea, but it sure didn't apply. Coach Rajah made sure of that.

We took a few more shots on Victoria's net. But it was really cold. I started to shiver. Finally, even Victoria lost interest. I mumbled an excuse about having to go. To tell the truth, it wasn't the cold that made me quit. I just wished that things with Victoria and Willie would be the same as they had been in the fall.

To tell the truth, I wasn't even that excited about the playoffs with the Cougars.

# 8

# Dead Meat

During the warm-up before the first playoff game with the Cougars, Jamie Reisberry skated over to me and said: "You're dead, Henry."

I was standing in the goal crease with my pads and all my gear on. Before I had a chance to reply, he skated back to his own end. Some of our players looked at him funny, then continued to take practice shots.

It was noisy in the arena. All three of my grandfathers showed up. Grandpa Gord had brought enough cowbells for everybody, and a trumpet for himself. A lot of sound bounced off the cold walls.

"Don't let him get to you," Willie said. He had seen what happened. I just shrugged.

"Don't worry," I said. But still the whole thing made me nervous.

From the opening faceoff, the Cougars looked as though they wanted to run us out of the rink. Lars made the first rush. He went around Victoria as though she was standing still. Simon Lee, on right defence, played his position and came between Lars and me in goal. But then Lars turned Simon so inside out it looked as though he had his hockey socks on backwards.

Lars then let go a slapshot that caught me on the face mask.

Bells rang — and I don't mean the cowbells.

I'm sure Lars didn't do that on purpose. He's not like that. But for a moment I couldn't see. Then Lars grabbed the rebound. I saw that one coming just in time to kick out a pad.

Before our defence came back, Lars got a third shot away. I went down and grabbed at the puck. In the scramble, someone stepped on my glove hand. Simon then bodychecked Reisberry. He came down on top of me, stick first, crushing my chin guard into my throat pad.

When the whistle went, everyone tried to get untangled. Reisberry pushed his stick harder into my face as he got up.

"Sorry," he said, still on top of me, and looked at me with that fat little sick smile. He gave his stick one extra little push into my chin.

"That's enough of that," the referee said, lifting Reisberry by an elbow.

On the very next play on the faceoff, Reisberry came into my crease again. I gave him a nudge to get out of the way. He was blocking my view. He turned and without warning cross-checked me in the face.

I went down flat on my back. All I could see was a black blur as the puck sailed into the net.

The light came on and the Cougars started dancing and high-fiving. But the ref blew extra hard on the whistle, and waved her hands from side to side.

No goal.

She pointed one finger at Reisberry and skated to the penalty box. She held two fists in front of her with a jabbing motion, as though she was pretending to hold a stick.

Cross-checking. Two minutes.

"You okay, Jake?" Victoria asked. "He was after you pretty good."

"It's okay," I said. But I could still feel the spot on my neck where he had hit me.

On the power play, our team really took it to the Cougars. Carl did one of his rushes down the right side and was around the Cougars' goal before the defence knew he was in the neighbourhood. Jenny Lau came in on left wing just in time to take his pass.

She banged in his pass in a perfect play, even from what I could see two hundred feet away.

Bear Claws 1, Cougars 0.

For the first time ever we were ahead of the Cougars. I looked up to see all three of my grandfathers ringing bells like it was milking time back on the farm.

At the end of the first period I skated to the bench. Coach Rajah looked at me. "Are you all right to play the rest of the game?" he said.

I nodded. My jaw felt numb, like it did the time the dentist froze it to take out a tooth.

"That was a vicious jab," Rajah added. "There is no need for that."

We held the Cougars through the second period. But in the third, they started to come alive again. Our players looked tired.

"Hang in there, Jake," Victoria said after one scramble.

With about five minutes to go, the Cougars came in on a rush. Lars led the first rush — I remember that — and Reisberry must have been right behind him.

I stopped the first shot, but let a big rebound out. Somebody got that and fired it at me. I stuck out a pad, blocked it. Lars took the rebound behind the net. He passed out to the point.

Reisberry planted himself right in front of me. I peeked left and right, trying my best to see through all the arms and legs. Reisberry's hands and stick came right at my face. He had hit me once. I wasn't about to let him do it again.

I jerked back and rocked on my skates, flailing both my stick and catching arm trying to stay on my feet.

I had lost sight of the puck — but not for long. I heard the ping, as the puck bounced off the right post, followed by a shushing sound as it caromed into the net.

Cougars 1, Bear Claws 1.

Immediately, both Willie and Victoria were pointing at Reisberry, and skating after the ref. In the stands all three grandfathers were yelling and jumping and turning purple in the face.

"Interference!" Willie yelled. "Interference!"

"No goal, no goal, no goal!" yelled the grandfathers.

Victoria chased the ref to the scorekeeper box, making little cross-checking motions with her stick, trying to tell the ref that Reisberry had cross-checked me.

Parents and spectators supporting both sides were yelling and screaming. Arguments broke out.

The ref blew her whistle and pointed to centre ice. Face-off. Reisberry hadn't touched me, so I couldn't argue with the call.

Someone threw an orange on the ice near the centre line. The ref picked it up and skated with it to the scorekeeper bench. What happened then I'm not sure.

All I saw was Grandpa Gord with a bugle in his hand.

For all these games, he had been content to ring cowbells and yell loudly. Now, all of a sudden he had pushed himself near the penalty bench where the scorekeeper sat. When the ref bent over to drop the orange over the boards, Grandpa Gord stood up and let out a bugle blast right in her ear.

From my angle I could see he wasn't really all that close to the ref. He was loud, though. The blast from the bugle echoed off the rafters, off the concrete block walls, and rattled the glass along the boards.

The ref put her hands over her ears.

When the bugle blast had chased itself out of the rink one last time, Grandpa Gord lowered the bugle.

The ref pointed at Grandpa Gord as though he got a penalty. She signalled to the scorekeeper and said something to Grandpa Gord. Grandpa Gord said something back. The ref pointed to the exit, back to Grandpa Gord, then to the exit again.

And that's how one of my grandfathers got kicked out of the hockey game.

# 9

# No Cowbells

Even from the goal at the far end, I could see the arena manager leading Grandpa Gord out the door. I wasn't sure what had happened. With the score tied 1–1 and four minutes left in regulation time, I knew I had to focus.

The ref didn't waste time. When the door closed behind Grandpa Gord, she dropped the puck.

The stands stayed quiet. The Cougars held their mouths tight in a grim line like zippers. You could see cold anger in their eyes.

I've said that Willie wasn't a fast centreman. He won the faceoff, all right, but before he could do anything with it, Lars had taken the puck back. Morley Davidson stopped him, and shot it behind the Cougars' net.

When Victoria pitched in to forecheck, Willie dropped back to left defence. She took the puck behind the Cougars' net, ragged the puck back and forth, looking for a clear pass. The Cougars' goalie shifted from side to side, worrying about when she would try to come out.

Instead, she finally spied Willie just inside the blue line and hit him with a perfect pass. Willie slapped the puck back and forth twice on his stick and looked for a shot. He bent forward to put some oomph behind it.

He was too late. Lars, ever on the prowl, had skated out full speed toward him. Lars poke-checked the puck from Willie's stick. It bounced off the boards, around Willie like a bouncing shot on a pool table. Willie had a good chance to stop him then with a bodycheck. But he didn't. Instead, he stabbed at the puck, missed, and Lars was off like he smelled free popcorn.

Lars was in full flight when he got the puck free; everyone on our team had been expecting Victoria's shot, so they were going the other way, toward the Cougars' net, hoping good things would happen. They didn't. Lars hit the red line before our team started back.

When he hit the blue line, I drifted forward high out of the crease, hoping to cut off the angle. By the time he lifted his head and saw me coming, it was too late for him to shift. We collided like two freight trains. Only I was a softer, more padded train.

We both went down.

Lars sprawled onto his stomach. His momentum kept him going, face down, spinning like a spiral galaxy right into the end boards with a gentle thunk.

The puck followed him, moving slowly. I swung at it, holding firmly to my stick. I sure didn't want to hit Lars with my stick again.

Flat on the ice, from behind the net, Lars swept his stick along the ice in front of the goal just enough to deflect the puck over the line.

Cougars 2, Bear Claws 1.

Our team tried for the next two minutes but it wasn't enough. When the final horn sounded, the Cougars piled around their goalie and everybody hugged Lars.

Our team stomped off to the dressing room. Nobody said much. There wasn't much to say.

# 10

# More Practice

At practice the next day I told Coach Rajah about Reisberry's threat.

"Watch him in tomorrow's game," is all Coach Rajah would say. "It may be all talk. He's smart enough to try to intimidate you, and mean enough to make you worry. And as we've seen, he doesn't forget."

"Yeah, he skates like an elephant," said Simon Lee. He made plodding noises something like an elephant might make on skates — if you have a good imagination. Which Simon doesn't.

"For an elephant, he went around Willie pretty good a couple of times," replied Tyler Wilson.

"Ask Jake, there, about how it feels to be cross-trunked," said Carl Biro. "He got whacked hard more than once."

Coach Rajah lifted his hands for silence. "Okay, ladies and gentlemen," he said. "We've got an hour on the ice today. We want to make the most of it. There are a few plays we need to work on. The whole season rests on how you do tomorrow night."

"Are we done for the season if we lose?" asked Tyler.

Before Rajah could answer, the door burst open — there's no other word for it. In marched Grandpa P.J. followed by Grandpa Ron.

"Coach Rajah, could you use a couple of old guys to help you out there today?" Grandpa P.J. asked as he strode through the dressing room door.

Both Grandpa P.J. and Grandpa Ron had skates slung over one shoulder, the way some players used to in old pictures. They propped their sticks in the rack by the door.

Coach Rajah looked from one to the other and then back at me. I slunk down a bit, trying not to show how embarrassed I was.

"You mean coaching help?" said Rajah, scratching his head. "I dunno." I could tell he was trying to find a way to say no without hurting their feelings. Coach Rajah is like that.

"Couple of old guys who used to play some pretty good hockey," said Grandpa P.J. "Give the kids some advice, help, maybe some inspiration, that sort of thing."

They took seats on the bench. Grandpa P.J. looked over at Tyler. "I heard you ask that question. Are you out if you lose tomorrow night?" he said. "That's what best-of-three series means. When you're one game down, you have your backs to the wall. It's do or die. Now or never."

"Good stuff," said Coach Rajah. "This team is always short of clichés."

"You mean we can help?" asked Grandpa Ron.

Rajah smiled. "Sure. And after, maybe you could split some kindling for the hot stove league. You didn't bring cowbells, did you?"

"That's Jake's other grandfather," said Simon.

"No, no," said Grandpa Ron. "No cowbells. But I could get some ..."

"Ron," said Grandpa P.J. "He's pulling your leg."

Grandpa Ron nodded, said, "Oh," and began to lace his skates.

"Who's the goalie next game?" asked Grandpa P.J. When he bent over to lace his skates his face turned purple. His hair fell down over his face. You could see his bald spot.

Grandpa Ron started talking to Morley and Simon, who sat beside him. "I went to the same high school as Bobby Hull," he said. "And I played on the provincial Juvenile 'D' finalists," he added. "You guys gotta work on your wrist shots."

Morley is a very patient guy and would never hurt any-body's feelings. He looked at Grandpa Ron and his odd socks, and he said, "Who is Bobby Hull?"

Grandpa Ron looked at him with one eyebrow up, the other down, and both eyes wide in astonishment. "These kids today," he said to no one in particular. "Bobby Hull. NHL scoring leader seven different times. Twelfth on the overall scoring list. I ever tell you guys I went to school ..."

Everybody started laughing, especially Rajah. Grandpa Ron looked around as though he had missed the joke.

"What's so funny?"

"Yeah, I think you told us that before," said Willie.

                              * * *

On the ice at practice, Grandpa P.J. hovered by Victoria's shoulder while she warmed up.

"Stick on the ice," he said. "Keep it flat. That's it."

I was dressed for my position at left defence. Coach Rajah had turned all the defence players to him.

"Wrist shot," he kept repeating. "You want to know where that shot is going, wrist it."

Several of us tried wrist shots. Willie got the best away, but from the point even his shot was a high floater that I could have plucked out of the air without my goalie stuff on.

"That's good, that's good," Grandpa Ron repeated. "Now see if you can get some oompf into it."

"The oompf," said Willie, "comes from the slapshot."

"But the slapshot," began Grandpa Ron — and I knew what he was going to say before he said it — "You never know where it is going to go."

"And about the bodycheck," said Grandpa P.J. to Willie. "Try a hip check. Something like this." He skated backwards with his hip thrust out until he bumped into the boards and fell down.

"Like that?" asked Willie.

"Something like that," said Grandpa P.J., brushing himself off. "Of course, you got to go to the guy, not the boards. Besides, any guy you hit has to be softer than the boards."

"Unless he's moving sixty miles an hour," said Willie.

For practice, Coach Rajah had put targets on one net: one each in the top and bottom corners. Grandpa Ron skated over and tapped the targets.

"Show me," he said, almost losing his balance on his skates.

Morley lined four pucks up just inside the blue line. He drew back his stick and let go four slapshots: one, two, three, four, one after the other.

Ping! Ping! Ping! Ping!

He caught the targets, one at a time: top left, top right, bottom right, bottom left.

Grandpa Ron seemed almost disappointed.

"Oh," he said.

At the far end, Grandpa P.J. was giving Victoria some practice shots. Victoria was blocking each easily. I skated over to watch.

"Pads together," Grandpa P.J. kept repeating. "A good shot will catch that space between your skates if you do that. No, no, no."

Victoria kept stopping everything he shot but he wasn't satisfied.

"A good attacker will pick any spot you leave," he instructed her. "Here, let me show you."

He skated in slowly, a slow-motion one-on-one with a goalie. He tried to deke Victoria out of position, but she wouldn't fall for it. She stopped his shot easily and steered it off to the side.

"Let me try that again."

This time Grandpa P.J. sped up a bit. I have to admit he could really move, for an old guy, and he did have a pretty good shot. He faked a low wrist shot at the five-hole. Victoria blocked it easily.

"You were saying?" said Coach Rajah, with a smile.

"She's doing pretty good," said Grandpa P.J. "Especially for a girl." I looked over at Victoria. She glared at me with that look she gets when she is playing goal and nobody is going to score. Several team members booed.

"And these guys have pretty good slapshots," added Grandpa Ron. "Pretty darned good. Even the girls."

"Well, that's great," said Coach Rajah. "We've worked on that all season. And thanks. These guys needed a bit of a break from our tough workouts. But right now we're going to have some scrimmage. So if you'll be so kind ..."

"You aren't inviting us to play?" asked Grandpa P.J., disappointed.

"We won't bodycheck hard," said Grandpa Ron, who hadn't played in fifty years.

"Sorry, guys," said Coach Rajah. "I'm the only one who knows CPR here. And I have no ambition of going mouth to mouth with either of you."

He grinned widely, but I don't think either of my grandfathers got his joke. I really don't.

# 11

# Icing But No Cake

Skating out on clean ice at the start of a sudden-death game is a thrill. We were playing at the Courtice Arena, on Pad B, which has a larger ice surface. It is an Olympic-size rink. We hadn't played on it all year.

"It's huge!" said Willie, before stepping on the ice.

"An extra fifteen feet wide, that's all," said Coach Rajah. "If I'd known we were going to get this pad we would have done some special prep."

"The Cougars'll kill us on this!" said Tyler. "Their fast guys will walk around us."

Coach Rajah knocked a knuckle gently on his helmet. "Think positive thoughts," he said. "This just means you'll have more room to catch them."

Tyler thought about that for a moment, before he said, "Oh."

The big overhead lights reflected on the shimmering ice. We skated a couple of laps on our end. Willie started to take warm-up shots on Victoria. He tried to pick the corners, the way Morley did, but he could only come close. Morley took over, picking the corners: top right, top left, bottom left, bottom right. Victoria looked ready.

She still wouldn't look at me, except a couple of times in

the dressing room. Then, her eyes had challenged me, as though she were saying, "I'll show you who should be the full-time goalie for this team."

In the stands — which were now full with parents, grand-parents and friends — Grandpa Ron and my father sat with my mother and Fred. I couldn't see Grandpa P.J. I couldn't *hear* Grandpa Gord. Usually, his cowbells clanged every time he moved in his seat.

Still in the warm-up, I was skating along the centre red line when Jamie Reisberry coasted up on my right shoulder.

"Tonight we get revenge."

He was gone before I could say anything back.

The referee tooted the whistle. The game was ready to start. I was playing left defence in the starting lineup. The rest of the team had settled on the bench when I heard the bells arrive.

I looked over to the main door. Grandpa Gord stood framed in the doorway. He had a harness of sleighbells around his mid-dle. As he walked he sounded like a reindeer left over from Christmas. The arena manager was standing in front of him, blocking his way. She was shaking her head firmly from side to side.

From the distance, and separated by the glass, I couldn't hear what was being said. Grandpa Gord's mouth was gaping over and over, as though he were saying, "But, but, but, but …" The arena manager was having none of it. She pointed firmly to the door.

I didn't see any more. The whistle tooted, the puck was dropped, and the game was on.

Right from the start we could see the advantage the bigger ice gave to the Cougars.

Lars beat Willie in the opening faceoff, and kicked the puck to Reisberry on his right. I mentioned before about Reisberry being a big, dumb guy. What I should add is that he is a big, dumb *fast* guy. He came straight down the boards toward me.

I sprinted hard to build speed and turned with him, skating backward, trying to keep between him and the goal.

Skating backward I knew I could not outrace Reisberry. Now, he had more room on the bigger ice. He took two extra strides to get by me and cut to the inside.

By the time he crossed the faceoff circle, I was a stride behind him. At the inside edge of the circle he drew back for a slapshot. I could see Victoria drift out to challenge him. Lars was coming in on the other side with no one near.

When Reisberry drew his stick back, I reached forward and got my stick in front of his. His shot was weak and slid along the ice and missed the goal.

That first period was the longest I can remember.

The Cougars' fast stick-handlers used the extra ice for end-to-end rushes. When we did get the play to their end, their players would pick up the puck behind the net and skate through our team like food through a goose.

We did have one star, though.

Wave after wave of Cougars kept flying in, peppering Victoria with low shots, high shots, left, right, slapshots, wrist shots, rebounds, you name it.

For a whole period and a half she stopped them all.

On the bench near the end of the second period, Coach Rajah sat Willie and me side by side.

"Switch positions next shift," he said.

"What do you mean?" Willie asked.

"Just that. Switch. Willie, you play left defence. Jake, I want you at centre."

"But …" was all Willie and I got out.

"No 'buts.' Coach's orders. I likely should have made that

change earlier this season. Willie, you've got size to keep things clear in front of Victoria. Jake, you can skate faster forward than backward. I want you out there back-checking these guys. If they're going to walk in and take shots, I don't want them getting a second chance. Got that?"

We both nodded.

All through this, Coach Rajah kept lifting his baseball cap, his black hair reflecting the light. The tighter the game got, the more nervous he got and the more often he lifted that hat. But no matter how tense things got, he insisted on our line rotation. Everybody got equal ice time.

Once, earlier in the season, when Tyler had referred to Joe and Aki as the defence on our third line, he had pulled everybody up sharply. "We have no third line," he said. "We have three first lines."

Joe and Aki were on defence when the Cougars finally scored. Lars had broken in to the right of Victoria. Aki had tried to ride him off into the corner, but Lars just kept going, came right around from behind the net and flipped a high shot at Victoria from the crease. Any goalie will tell you that's a tough one to judge. It's never a hard shot. It's more of a flip. But it comes almost from a goalie's feet, just as you're coming across and trying to see where the puck carrier is, and if he is going to pass it out.

She shied from the shot, straightening up while the puck went in over her shoulder.

The Cougars led 1–0.

In the third period we began to get our bearings back. For one thing, I'm sure that the Cougars had skated some of the spring out of their legs. For another, the Bear Claws began to remember that hockey is a team sport.

We still couldn't outskate some of those Cougars. But our passes started to look as though we had Velcro on our sticks. We began to realize that we could pass faster than any player could skate.

Midway through the third period, we were dominating the play. The crowd got noisier. Not as noisy as it could have been, since Grandpa Gord and his cowbells were nowhere to be heard. Strangely, I missed them. Halfway through the third period I looked up from the bench and saw Grandpa P.J. come in. I felt relieved.

That was when we almost blew the whole game.

Lars won the faceoff, tipped the puck between his legs to his defence. Harvey Hyndman snapped a pass to Reisberry, who was motoring down the boards to my left. For a big, stupid guy he could really move. He had cut by Sandie before she had fully turned. Even Morley Davidson, the defenceman nobody gets around, couldn't make it over from his position.

So Reisberry came bearing down on Victoria. Morley skated hard to get back. I knew then that if Reisberry tried to deke around Vickie, Morley might be able to take him.

But Reisberry stepped easily around Morley. Then suddenly Willie appeared as though out of nowhere, skating hard to get back in position. He came between Reisberry and the goal, lined up for a perfect bodycheck.

Instead, Willie reached out with his stick to get the puck. Reisberry deked once, shifted to the left and let a shot go that hit Vickie on the left shoulder.

"Play the man," Rajah said to Willie at the end of the shift.

The next shift, I took the faceoff just outside our blue line. I got the puck back to Willie, who took three strides to the centre line and slapped a hard shot toward the goal. When I saw him wind up, I headed full speed over the blue line.

I got in behind the Cougars' defence. When the puck ricocheted off the boards, I was the first one there. I stopped hard, sending a shower of snow in the air. I grabbed the puck and ragged it, waiting.

Harvey made the mistake of coming behind the net to get me. I popped out the other side.

Willie, playing left defence, saw me coming. He roared in from the point and took my pass, while I headed back out to the point to cover his position. It's a good thing I did. Behind me, I heard Willie's shot go *Ping*! off either the post or the cross-bar.

The rebound came out almost to the blue line. Lars pounced on the puck like a sled dog after raw meat, and took off with it. Luckily, I was three strides ahead. I cut in toward centre to head him off. He shifted and got around me, but that shift cost him a stride. Plus, I had come at him from an angle, just the way Coach Rajah taught us. I turned to my right and came at him again. This meant he had to beat me again. He did — right on our blue line. Lars shifted right and then left, leaving me with my underwear hanging on the blue line.

But that meant Lars's other winger, Alvin Sararis, crossed the blue line offside.

I looked up at the clock. Three minutes.

Reisberry skated over. "Three more minutes, Henry," he said.

I turned to him, not sure of what I was hearing.

"In three minutes, your season is over," he said. "I've still got a little revenge to collect." He pushed at me with his stick, challenging the way you see the pros do it when they go nose to nose.

The ref skated between us and pointed to the faceoff circle outside the blue line and tooted the whistle.

Lars beat me in the faceoff, but I regained the puck from Alvin. Carl Biro picked up my pass and headed down the right-wing boards. I headed for the net — hoping good things would happen.

I shifted back and forth in front of the Cougars' net while
Carl struggled to keep the puck in the corner. Reisberry arrived
and tried pushing me out of the way.

Jenny Lau was playing left wing. She had moved in to help
Carl in his corner. Reisberry slipped around to head me off. I
spun around, between him and the goal, trying to get to Carl,
who was struggling with a Cougar defence player. Reisberry
rode me off to the boards and wouldn't let me join the play.

Next thing I knew I was backed against the boards. Reisberry lifted his stick and gave me a fierce cross-check to the
throat. I mean fierce, like for a moment I couldn't breath or
swallow.

When someone does that, you want to get even. Really you do.
I know I wanted to. The only problem was, I couldn't. As I sank to
my knees I saw the ref's hand go up for a delayed penalty.

With a delayed penalty, we had a guaranteed ride: the play
would continue while we had the puck. As soon as a Cougar
touched the puck, play would stop. Rajah had coached us to
watch for this. It gave us a chance to pull the goalie for an extra
attacker — without risk. Of course, if the ref thought I was
injured she would whistle the play right away. Knowing this, I
struggled to my feet, although what I really wanted to do was
lie there and try to escape from the pain. Somehow, I saw Victoria scrambling for the bench at full speed.

Teams often pull a goalie in the last minute of play. But with
that there is always a risk, because the other team can shoot the
puck into the empty net. With a delayed penalty, you get the extra
attacker — and the only risk is if we shoot the puck into our own
net. Once the other team touches the puck, the play stops.

So, as Victoria headed for the bench, I headed for the corner to help Carl keep the puck. I scooped it up by his skate and
looked for a play. Jenny was parked in front of the goal waiting

for a pass or rebound, but was pretty well covered. Then I spotted Morley, who had come on as the extra attacker.

I passed up the centre as he came roaring in.

He one-timed a slapper that rang off the goalpost and out to the circle. Reisberry picked it up and the ref whistled the play down.

Two and a half minutes left — two with a power play.

Coach Rajah signalled for a time out.

# 12

# Icing Takes the Cake

When we skated back to the bench, Coach Rajah held out his clipboard. "Gather round, team," he said, and we all shifted so everyone could see. "Nice eyes on that delayed call, Vickie," he said. Victoria smiled through her face mask.

"Listen, everybody. This is the best chance you'll have. Tie the score now, and who knows what we can do in overtime. Willie, I want you to use that slapshot you have. Morley, I'm putting you out in the first change. Same reason. And keep control. They're going to play kitty-bar-the-door, and hope for a quick break. We can't give them that chance." He paused. "Questions?"

Carl raised a hand. "Why not put Willie and Morley out together?"

Rajah bounced a roll of tape off Carl's helmet. "We're not going to break up our rotation now," he said. "If we get a chance again to pull the goalie, though, we will."

\* \* \*

My legs by now had begun to feel like overcooked noodles — weak and rubbery. A look at the other faces on the bench told me everybody felt the pace.

The ref tooted the whistle to signal it was time to drop the puck. Todd took the first shift, centring between Tyler and Karmia Brown, with Morley and Sandie on defence.

Morley must have had six chances: one missed the net, one hit a post, the Cougars' goalie caught one, one hit a skate and went upstairs, and one hit Todd in the back. None went in.

In the next shift, David Wrigley took a pass right on the edge of the crease. He couldn't get his stick on it, and the chance dribbled away.

We did everything but score.

Our line came on to take a faceoff with thirty seconds left in the penalty — and one minute left in the game.

The faceoff was to the left of the Cougars' goal. I got set when Morley skated over from the bench and took a position to my left directly in the slot.

I queried him with my eyes. *"What's going on?"* Morley shifted his eyes to our end of the rink, where the net stood empty. Vickie was on the bench.

The penalty gave us a one-person advantage. Pulling our goalkeeper gave us an extra player — and an empty net. There was no room for mistakes. Since the Cougars had a penalty and were one player short, they could shoot the puck to our end without being called back. That meant they could shoot at that empty net any time they got the puck — with no danger.

On the other hand, we had two more skaters than they did — with the faceoff in their end.

Morley and Willie crept into the top of the circle on each side. The wingers dropped back to the point, ready to come in fast, but also ready with their speed to head off any possible break.

With seconds ticking away, I grabbed the puck behind the net and tried to stuff it. No go. But the puck stayed loose. I grabbed it again and threaded a pass to Morley, who rushed in.

From twelve feet out Morley let one go that was so fast it should have counted as a first-period goal. He had half an empty net to shoot at, a shot labelled for the right spot — when Lars dropped to the ice in front of him and took the full blast on the back of his legs.

I am sure that had he time to plan it, Lars would have preferred to stop that one shin pads first. As it was, the puck went *thunk*!, kind of softly, and there was no rebound. Lars tried to either cover the puck or clear it, I'm not sure which. He wasn't sure, either. He sat up and felt under him for the puck. In doing so, he lifted enough to free the puck.

I grabbed it and took off.

I circled behind the net and flipped a pass right up the centre to where Willie was supposed to be. Or where I thought Willie was supposed to be.

He wasn't.

The puck drifted straight up the centre, over the blue line and out.

At that moment — at that precise moment — Reisberry stepped out of the penalty box. Four strides and he picked up the puck, with no one between him and the empty net at our end of the rink.

I put my head down and started skating, but when you are seventy-five feet behind that's not going to do much good.

I could almost hear Reisberry laugh as he grabbed that puck, reaching out with his long arm, pulling it in. He took two more strides, cocked his stick back and, just this side of centre ice, let go a long shot.

Straight down the centre.

We watched in horror as the puck dropped inside our blue line, did a little pixie-dance as it slid along the ice toward our empty net.

# 13

## Cowbell Call

The puck continued to rotate on its edges down the ice. Reisberry raised his arms in victory. You could hear everyone else in the arena suck in a big breath.

From my angle I thought I saw the puck go in. But then it slid past the post, making a little bumping sound as it bounced off the boards at the far end.

Icing.

The linesman whistled the play dead. Reisberry dropped his arms, sagging visibly. The arena crowd breathed. On our bench, everyone exhaled, sat down and sighed once more.

Reisberry had shot from his own side of centre ice. Since the penalty was over, that's icing. The call gave us a faceoff in the Cougars' end. Now we were at even strength. I looked back at the bench. Coach Rajah had kept Victoria out of the goal. He didn't change shifts. We were to stay on until the end — which gave us thirty seconds to tie the score or the Bear Claws were done for the year.

I moved into the circle to take the faceoff. I glanced over my shoulder to check where our players were.

When the puck dropped, Lars and I pushed against each other so hard neither of us could move. The puck stayed motionless at our feet. I could feel my strength draining.

Finally I got my right skate on the puck and kicked it back to Morley. His shot hit someone on the way in and never got to the net. Carl Biro tried to shoot, but someone lifted his stick.

I joined the scramble in front of the net. Everything was a tangle of legs and arms. I was knocked off my feet. Morley got one shot away but missed the net. The rebound came right back out. Lars turned and slapped at it but missed. I flipped a shot but the goalie blocked it.

The rebound lay in the crease. The whole game now moved in slow motion; the goalie, eyes fixed on the puck, dropping to smother it; Jenny Lau, her brown eyes flashing, reaching toward the puck; Lars on his stomach, flailing, too far away.

Someone kicked it and the puck rolled toward the goal line, turned on its edge and rolled some more.

From my left a big player loomed.

Reisberry skated in hard from the left faceoff circle. He caught me with a cross-check in the back between the shoulder blades. I went down — but so did Reisberry, his momentum carrying him past me. He slid face first into his own goal, taking everything with him: his stick, his goalie, Jenny Lau, part of a linesman — and the puck.

The ref's hand went into the air, and pointed firmly down to the Cougars' goal.

Score!

The stands erupted.

Cougars 1, Bear Claws 1.

That meant overtime.

The pain in my shoulders was a small price to pay.

People in the stands continued to yell, and stamp, and clap. We had heard that before, but something was missing. Then I realized why.

No cowbells. With Grandpa Gord banned from the game,

for the first time all year there were no cowbells to celebrate a goal.

* * *

With the drop of the puck in overtime, the pace of the game was faster than anything we had ever played before.

On the bigger surface, the Cougars, with their speed and our tired legs, had the advantage. They used it.

For most of the game, the crowd had been quiet. I hadn't realized the effect Grandpa Gord's bells had on both sides until they weren't there. About three minutes into overtime, in the sliver of silence that echoed from the rink's walls just before a faceoff, a single voice rang out:

"COWBELLS! COWBELLS! COWBELLS!"

It was Grandpa P.J., standing, his hands cupped over his mouth, bellowing like an angry bull:

"COWBELLS! COWBELLS! COWBELLS!"

Now there were two voices. Then three, four, more.

The parents and fans of the Bear Claws picked up the chant. I looked over at our bench, embarrassed. But to my surprise, every player on our bench had joined in:

"COWBELLS! COWBELLS! COWBELLS!"

Even Coach Rajah, his leather lungs at work, had cupped his hands and added his voice.

"COWBELLS! COWBELLS! COWBELLS!"

The chant sent shivers up my spine. I felt a small lump in my throat. I was proud of my grandfathers. Proud of their silly antics. Proud of their support of me, of the team.

I knew we couldn't let them down.

I skated over to Willie. He, too, had fire in his eyes I had never seen before.

From the faceoff, I took Lars with the body and hooked a pass back to Willie. He wound up and let a slapshot go.

It went in head-high, but so wide of the goal that the Cougars' goalie had time to turn and take a sip from his water bottle.

But Carl trapped the puck in the far corner and got it back to Simon on the blue line. Simon hesitated, passed it cross-rink to Willie again. Willie slapped another one knee-high that scooted by the far corner. I was perched just outside the crease and took a swipe at it as it went by. I missed.

The crowd groaned, sort of an "Uhnnnnnnnnnnnnnnnnn," that trailed off. From the stands came another single voice, not quite so strong:

"Wrist it! Wrist it!" Grandpa Ron shouted.

From behind the net I fed the puck back to Willie again. This time he did get a quick wrist shot away. You could see it float all the way in. The Cougars' goalie nabbed it easily with his glove hand.

Coach Rajah kept the line changes fast. He had to, so we could keep up the fast pace. Every line came off a shift in less than a minute, sucking air like there wasn't much left.

We had our third overtime shift with about thirty seconds left in the four-on-four. From a face-off just outside the Cougars' blue line, I fed Jenny a neat pass. She drifted in almost halfway before she let a high one go. The Cougars' goalie used his blocker to steer the puck into the corner.

I outhustled Harvey Hyndman and got the puck. In the stands now, they were still chanting, "COWBELLS! COW-BELLS! COWBELLS!" and stamping their feet in rhythm.

Reisberry came at me behind the net at full speed, his stick high and hate in his eyes. At that moment I knew I had him. I pivoted with the puck, used my body to block Lars, and threaded a pass to Jenny, who now was all alone in front of the goal crease.

She made no mistake, flipping the puck into the top right corner for the winning goal.

The stands went wild, with half the people cheering wildly and the other half sitting on their hands.

For the first time all season we had beaten the Cougars. We had tied the series at one game each.

# 14

## Grace Note

It's called grace note," Grandpa Gord said. With his fiddle he played easily over the four bars I had been messing up. "It's sort of like an extra little note inserted quickly. To deflect the ear from what it expects. Listen, and then try it again."

He fingered the fiddle quickly with his huge, quick hands, twisting the bow just so to squeeze in that extra note. He did it without a change in beat.

I tried again. Really I did. But every time I got the extra note in I messed up the timing on the notes that followed. If I got the timing right in the grace note, it squeaked, squawked, or soured.

"It's like a sixteenth note just slid in," Grandpa Gord repeated.

Nanny Joyce stopped chording on the keyboard. "It's coming," she said. Which is when I knew it was, because she is always right. "Just don't rush it. It will come."

"When?" I asked.

"Your brain will figure it out," added Grandpa Gord.

"I think that's enough for today," said Nanny Joyce.

Grandpa Gord made a brushing motion with the back of his hand. "So skedaddle. What time is your game tomorrow?"

"Four o'clock."

"I'll be there."

I looked at him, pretending a frown. He held up a hand: "No bugles this time. Just my cowbells. Well, maybe a few more cowbells. But the arena manager said I would be allowed in. If I promise to behave. My suspension was for only one game."

The doorbell rang.

Grandpa P.J. stuck his head in the door.

"Is it safe for the auxiliary coach to come in?" he asked. He turned to me. "There are a couple of kids out there looking for somebody to play road hockey."

"I'm on my way," I replied. "You coming to my game tomorrow?"

"Your Grandpa Ron's coming, too," Grandpa P.J. replied. "I wouldn't miss it."

"They tell me you missed most of the last game, too," said Grandpa Gord, "What happened to you?"

Grandpa P.J. looked sheepish. "Wrong game," he said, after a pause.

"Wrong game?" said Grandpa Gord, impishly.

"I went to pad 'A' — where they usually play. There was a game on, and the sweaters looked pretty much the same ..."

"You watched the wrong game for two and a half periods? Didn't you find it strange that you couldn't see your own grandson?" asked Grandpa Gord.

"Don't bug me," replied Grandpa P.J. "And it was only a period and a half. Out on the ice with the helmets and everything, all the kids look the same."

"Is that the practiced eye of a veteran goalie?" asked Grandpa Gord. He gave me an exaggerated wink.

"Well, that was a mistake," said Grandpa P.J. "At least they didn't bar me from the arena."

"That," said Grandpa Gord, "was a misunderstanding between the arena manager and a deaf referee."

"That referee wasn't deaf," I said.

"She is now," said Grandpa P.J. "In one ear, anyway."

"But the main thing is, everything is fine," said Grandpa Gord. "They're going to let me back in for the final game."

I finished lacing up my in-line skates. "Can I leave now?" I asked. "Before you two start making serious noise? I want to get some road hockey in before dinner."

"Scoot," they said together.

Out on the road, Victoria and Willie were playing shots-on. Willie was peppering slappers from six metres out. Victoria was dressed in her full road hockey goalie equipment. She was grabbing Willie's shots okay — those that were on the net, and many were.

"Mind if I join?" I asked. Three months before, I would not have asked. But since Christmas, Victoria had not been exactly friendly. Willie just tried hard not to take sides, which meant he didn't say much.

"Whatever," Victoria said.

I grabbed the loose tennis ball and ragged it back and forth. "Look," I said. "I wasn't the one who wanted to change things. Just because your grandparents gave you a crap-load of equipment for Christmas doesn't mean I should stop playing goal."

"No need to be vulgar," said Victoria.

I slapped the tennis ball back and forth and walked slowly up to the goal. When I got to within Victoria's reach I faked a movement. She moved, and I flipped a shot almost straight up under her left arm into the net.

"Your weak spot," I said, trying not to sound triumphant.

Victoria only glared.

"He's right, Vickie. You're hitching up your skirt," Willie said, after a pause.

Since it was unusual for Willie to butt in, both Victoria and I stared at him.

"On that shot," Willie said. "You did the same thing yester-day on the first goal. It was like you were hitching up your skirt. With that flip shot coming up at you, you pulled back and up — away from the shot instead of into it."

Victoria mimed her reaction, rising on her toes and pulling her face away from an imaginary shot. "Yeah, like that," Willie said.

"I see," Victoria said.

"But 'hitching up your skirt'?" I asked.

Willie came as close to blushing as ice is to hockey. "I dunno. Guess it doesn't really fit. But remember when the teacher read us the book *Huck Finn*, how when he was dressed as a girl and that lady threw something to him, he caught it by putting his knees together? And the woman knew he was a boy, because a girl would have caught it in her skirt. Different reac-tion."

"What's that got to do with the goal I let in?" said Victoria. "Like, duh. When was the last time you saw me wear a skirt?"

"Nothing, and yeah, it's dumb," Willie said. "But it's just that your reaction to that one shot is wrong. That's the only point I'm trying to make."

"So I should change my reaction." From Victoria it was a statement, not a question.

"Coach Rajah's been working at us all year trying to get us to drop old bad habits," he said. "Seems like that might be just a bad habit."

Victoria thought for a moment, moving her head from side to side. "Mmm. Yeah, you're likely right."

Willie and I took turns flipping shots at Victoria from close in. At first she continued to flinch back, away from the shot. Not that she was afraid of it.

"I need to see it first," she said. "Then I can react."

"React first, see later," said Willie. "This close, you won't see it. Even though these are not hard shots."

"Try again," she said.

I did. She flinched again. This time, though, instead of flinching up and back from the shot she moved out and toward me. This cut off the angle so there was little to shoot at.

"That's better."

We tried variations of this same shot until Victoria was blocking them all.

Finally she said, "Okay, I think I got that. But now that Willie is playing the point, maybe we should practice some slapshots."

"Good idea," I said. "Your slappers still make Grandpa Ron look like he knows something about the game."

"Snigglarf," said Willie.

He let go a slapshot that, had it been on goal, would have gone in the net, even if Victoria got in front of it. But it didn't, and she didn't, and the ball soared down the street, bounced a few times and rolled onto Mr. Valentine's lawn.

"Fetch," I said. "Street rules: you chase your own."

"Maggotbarf," said Willie. But he skated down the street to get the ball.

"You played good last game," I said to her. "Real good."

Victoria lifted her face mask. "Thanks. I think." She took a sip of water from the bottle on top of the net and adjusted her gloves. "You realize you never call me by name?" she said.

"What?"

"You never call me by my name. Willie does. Everybody else on the team does. They say, 'Nice game, Vickie.' Or, 'Good try, Vickie.' But you don't. Even when you say something nice, like you just did."

I didn't know how to respond to that.

Willie skated back up the street — without the tennis ball.

"Valentine's got it," he said.

"He must have a million of our balls," I said. "You think maybe he's got a backyard full of them?"

"Oh, man!" said Victoria. She threw down a real puck. "Try this," she said. "Only just don't expect me to stop it."

Willie backed up to the next driveway — about a blue line's distance from the goal. He swung his stick back and let a slapper go. It missed the net by a quarter mile. I relented and skated down the street to get the puck. It hadn't rolled as far as a ball would.

"Try again," I said. "See if you can hit Vickie."

He tried again. This time it was closer. I had stayed down the street to stop the puck and shoot it back. Just then Grandpa Ron and my dad pulled into the driveway.

"Do all your grandfathers come to your place at the same time?" asked Vickie.

"Sometimes," I said. "Like today. Likely tomorrow after the game."

"You," Vickie said, "have a weird family. Nice, but weird."

Grandpa Ron walked over. "Using the slapshot, I see," he said.

Willie tried not to wince. "I know, I know," he said. "I never know where it's going."

"You have good speed," he said. "You can score lots on that. But first maybe you need some help getting it on the goal."

Willie shrugged. "Sure."

Grandpa Ron pointed at me. "Jake. Move up here and stand by the edge of the goal. If Willie's shot misses, you see if you can knock it in."

"I don't get it," said Willie.

"It's called a deflection," said Grandpa Ron. "Jake stands in front of the goal, or beside it. If your shot misses, Jake tries to bat it into the goal."

"You mean, hit it while it's in the air?"

"Into the net, of course."

"Deflection," I said.

"Sometimes it's called a tip-in. You need quick hands but it gives the goalie no chance."

"Hey, that sounds cool," said Vickie, making a sour face.

"Thanks, Grandpa Odd Socks," Willie said.

"Welcome," he replied. "You just about ready to go?"

"We want to try to fit a movie in if we can," said my dad, who had been standing by, watching.

"Just want to say hi to the folks back in the house," said Grandpa Ron.

While Dad watched, we worked at the tip-in for a couple of dozen shots. It sounded like a good idea. But if Willie's slapshot was too fast for most goalies, it was also too fast for me to tip in. I could see the shot all right, but getting my stick on it was hard. When I did, getting the puck to go where I wanted was even harder.

We were about ready to give up when my three grandfathers and Nanny Joyce and my mother came out.

Grandpa P.J. took a look at the puck. "Where's the tennis ball?" he asked. "Lose it?"

"Mr. Valentine kept it," I said, "Again."

"He's done that before?" asked my dad.

"All the time," I said.

"That old bugger," said my father. "Let me have a chat with him." He started to march off down the street.

"Now Dann," said my mother, "don't be pulling one of your stunts."

"Stunts? Someone stole our son's property!"

"Not Jake's," said Willie. "Vickie's."

"Same thing. I should stand by and do nothing?"

"Just remember we have to live with these neighbours."

Dad huffed from halfway down the street. Willie grunted something. He blasted another shot that zipped by the goalpost. I waved my stick at it but missed completely.

"Get your stick on it," said Grandpa Ron.

"Keep your stick on the ice," said Grandpa P.J., even though it was March, we were on the road, and the "ice" was just pavement. He spoke to Willie.

"Use the body, man," he said. "You got to learn to use the body."

Willie shrugged.

"No, I'm serious. Bodychecking is legal, check the rules. You have the size and strength. You don't have to hit or do anything mean. Just use your strength to ride Lars and what's his name, Reisberry, off the puck."

"But they played rep hockey," Willie said.

"They don't any more," said Grandpa P.J. "They only deserve the respect they earn. What they deserve tomorrow is a few good bodychecks from you." He tried to tweak Willie's nose but Willie was too tall.

Willie turned and tried another slapshot. Again I tried a deflection but missed.

"An eighth note," said Grandpa Gord.

"Huh?" I said. "What's fiddle music got to do with this?"

Grandpa Gord came over and took my stick. "I never played hockey," he said, "But this is a musical problem. You're trying to steer Willie's shot in the goal, right?"

"That's the idea," said Grandpa Ron. "That was *my* idea." He beamed.

"But it's like the grace notes," said Grandpa Gord. "Look at

Willie's swing. It's like a pendulum. So it's, backswing, kaw-zunk, zip, ting!" He made a rhythmic movement with his hands, sort of like holding a fiddle like it was a hockey stick.

"Kaw-zunk, zip, ting!" he repeated.

The weird thing is, I think I understood him.

"Try it again."

Willie wound up for another slapshot. It still didn't go in the net, but this time I got the edge of my stick on it.

"Better," said Vickie.

"Again."

I got more wood on the next one, although it still didn't score.

"Keep at it," said Grandpa Gord. "Your brain will figure it out."

Willie took a few more practice shots. I got so I could hit one in three. In goal, Vickie could follow Willie's shot in, although the only thing you could depend on was that he would miss the net. If I got a blade on it about a foot off the ground I could deflect it into the net behind her. She didn't have a chance.

We were about ready to wrap it up when I figured something out. I like to think, all by myself.

"Vickie, you've never played centre," I said.

She looked at me. "Well, like, duh. I'm left defence. When I'm not in goal."

"But the coach switched Willie and me last game. He's likely to keep Willie on left defence again. His point shots are murder. That would mean you would have to play centre."

She shrugged.

I continued. "And why am I practicing this deflection? If I'm in goal tomorrow I'll never get a chance to use it."

"So what are you saying, Jake?"

"You played so well last game," I paused. "Vickie." I looked at her seriously. "That's why we won. You have to play goal again tomorrow."

Vickie looked at me like I'd just handed her the Stanley Cup.

"And you play centre again! You did very well."

"We'll all talk to the coach before the game," I said. "I'm sure he'll go for it."

Vickie didn't say anything, but the way she shot the puck at me I knew she was pleased.

Dad came walking back up the street. Beside him was Mr. Valentine. Each had hold of one handle of a bushel basket. When they got up to us, the handle slipped from Dad's grasp and a basketful of tennis balls rolled out onto the street.

"Whoa!" said Willie. "That's a handful."

"I guess these belong to you," said Mr. Valentine, wiping a hand across his hawk-beaked nose. The balls rolled down the driveway into the street.

Vickie looked at him, and then at the balls rolling along the gutter.

"Not all of them. We lost some, but not *that* many."

Mr. Valentine furrowed his brow, trying to look fierce. He looked first at Vickie, then at me.

"Well, do you want them or not? I've been saving them for years, but if you want them, they're yours."

"For years?" said Willie.

"Think you're the only kid on the street?" replied Mr. Valentine.

We looked at the balls — there must have been a hundred or so — and suddenly Vickie began laughing. We all laughed, all but Mr. Valentine.

Finally, Vickie said, "Thanks, Mr. Valentine."

Dad lifted one hand. "But one more thing. Mr. Valentine said sometimes you guys chew up his lawn and flower beds with your skates."

"That's right. And it's got to stop."

We all looked at Willie. Willie looked up, right at Mr. Valentine.

"Sorry," Willie said. "We're all sorry. And I'll make sure these guys don't do it again."

"You make sure of that. I don't want you tearing up my tulips this spring." He turned and marched back down the street, his bushel basket dangling from one arm.

"That," said Willie, "is a grouchy old man."

"And what do you mean," said Vickie, "that you'd make sure we didn't chew up his lawn? You're the only one who chases balls down there."

Willie looked triumphant. "Not any more," he said. "From now on, we take turns, got it? You, me, then Jake. It's only fair."

"Maybe we don't need to chase them anymore," said Vickie, "until Mr. Valentine's basket gets full again."

We all laughed this time, even all three grandfathers, Nanny Joyce, and my dad. I don't think Mr. Valentine could hear us.

* * *

That night in the sports restaurant, my dad nudged me. He had sauce from the wings on his chin.

"I'm sorry I gave you a hard time over that New Year's tournament," he said.

"He thought I wouldn't understand," said Grandpa Ron, chewing on chicken.

"There was a day when you wouldn't have," said Dad.

"I guess I was kind of bratty," I said. "It's just that ..."

"Don't worry about it," said Dad, wiping the sauce off his chin with the napkin. "We both just proved we're people — we're not perfect."

"Give everybody a chance to learn," said Grandpa Ron. "I mean, what is more important to a Canadian, family or hockey? Used to be a day when I wouldn't go out in public until I found socks that matched."

"You don't have that problem anymore," I said.

# 15

# The Final

The Courtice Arena's Pad A was jammed to the rafters for the final game. Even from the dressing room before the game we could hear the buzz of the crowd in the stands. Grandpa Gord's cowbells tinkled gently, but you knew enough to expect something if we gave him a reason to make noise. Like if we scored.

Or better yet, if we won.

I shook the cobweb of those thoughts from my head. The last thing we needed, Coach Rajah had convinced us, was to be thinking *victory party* when what we should be thinking was *hockey*.

"Don't be daydreaming," he said in the dressing room. "Focus on the moment. Not the last play. Not the next play. Focus on the play you are making. Do it right, and the other things will come."

We got his message.

Vickie looked across the dressing room at me before she put on her helmet, mouth guard, and face mask. She smiled and gave me a thumbs up.

The two of us — three, actually, because Willie was there — had got to the dressing room early and talked to Coach Rajah about our suggestion to break the goalie rotation. I say *sugges-*

*tion* because Rajah was the kind of coach you could make suggestions to. If he thought they were good, you got to make them work. If he didn't think they were for the best of the team, he would say no.

This time he agreed.

For this game, Rajah locked the dressing room door before the game. Other times, he had let parents and friends into the room before the game.

This time: none.

I can't tell you what else Coach Rajah said to us in the dressing room before the game. It's a team secret.

I can tell you this: when we came out of that dressing room, we were ready for anything.

\* \* \*

When we stepped on the ice, the crowd applauded and cheered, and cowbells rang. Grandpa Gord had brought several sets. All the seats were filled. Parents were standing two-deep around the rink, and along the rail behind the seats in the stands.

"Let's give them their money's worth," Morley said, as we warmed up.

Vickie looked good during warm-up, kicking out shots from all angles.

Then she left the net and skated once around our end, adding extra stretches and skating backwards. While she did that, Willie took a couple of slappers from the blue line. I stood by the net and tried to slap them down, deflect them, anything.

You ever try to hit a bullet-like shot from thirty, forty feet away? It's not easy. I got wood on only two of the five before the ref tooted the whistle and we were ready for the opening faceoff.

* * *

From the faceoff, the Cougars pounced right away, using everything they could to get a jump on us early. It was as though the overtime from the previous game had continued.

Lars beat me cleanly on the opening faceoff, grabbed the puck, and headed straight in. Willie and Simon Lee lunged, trying to squeeze him. Lars flipped a pass to his right. Reisberry was coming in fast, took the pass in full flight and headed straight to the goal.

Both Willie and Simon were caught flat-footed. Sure, they had squeezed Lars out of the play, but they'd also given Reisberry a one-on-none.

Vickie coasted out to the top of the crease, glanced quickly to her right to see who Reisberry had with him. When she saw that he was alone, she stood her ground, waiting for the big guy to make the first move.

At the top of the circle Reisberry faked a shot. Vickie didn't fall for it. She followed him as he came across the front of the goal, sweeping away his scoring chances with her goal stick.

That's the way it was for most of the game.

They came at us time after time. We were reduced to playing defence — blocking shots, back-checking, clearing rebounds and letting Vickie do her job. For the first two periods their pressure looked like a power play, like they were playing keep-away with us.

Then we'd pounce on a mistake, or a bad bounce, and make a rush down to their end. Then Lars, or Reisberry, or one of their fancy skaters would return the rush and waltz in on Vickie alone.

"You keep letting them go in like that, one of them will score," Coach Rajah said at the end of the second period. "Keep on 'em." Of course, we knew that, and he knew that we knew that. Rajah was just nervous. We were all nervous.

Vickie kept us in the game. The score stayed 0–0 until halfway through the third period.

I was out on regular shift. By now, the Cougars' coach was playing Lars and Reisberry opposite Jenny and Carl and I all the time.

At centre ice, Lars pounced on a loose puck. Right away, his two wingers skated hard down each side. Willie had learned his lesson earlier, however, and took Lars out standing up. It was more like a push than a bodycheck, but Lars was out of the play. Willie poked the puck away and fed it to Simon.

Now we had three Cougar forwards going the wrong way. Simon passed the puck to me. I wheeled at centre and led a rush over the Cougars' blue line, with Simon and Willie following hard behind. The Cougars' defence players were out of position. I headed straight for the one Cougar between me and the goal.

As I got to him, I dropped a pass to Carl, who rang one off the goalpost. Jenny got the rebound, but the Cougar goalie kicked that out hard.

Too hard. It came almost out to the point, where Willie had taken his position. He coasted forward to the loose puck and lined up a slapshot that I am sure broke the speed of light.

Even better: For the first time that season he hit the goal.

The shot went over the goalie's shoulder on his glove side, and into the top corner.

1–0.

Bedlam on the ice, on the bench, and in the stands.

Cowbells. Shouts. Applause.

From somewhere, a bugle. Grandpa Gord blew it hard — but not in anyone's ear.

Again. And again.

Before she dropped the puck to resume play, the ref stared up at the stands to where Grandpa Gord and the rest of my family were still jumping. She didn't drop the puck until the bugle stopped.

We knew the Cougars would pour everything at us to tie the score.

They came flying down the left side, right side, up the centre. They did drop passes, fake passes, soft passes, hard shots. Vickie kicked out shots, challenged skaters, stoned Lars twice on breakaways, and robbed Reisberry of two I could not have stopped.

But through the third period we held that slim lead.

With two minutes to go, Lars charged in alone. He split the defence. When he still couldn't get a shot, he skated past the goal and came around from behind.

Vickie slid over to cover the wrap-around.

Again, Lars held the puck as though he had bubble-gummed it to his stick. As he came around to the edge of the crease he flipped a shot almost straight up.

Vickie didn't flinch, but continued across the goal and took the shot coolly with her glove hand.

With a minute to go we were still leading by that one goal. As expected, the Cougars pulled their goalie — and called for a time out.

"Don't get overanxious, now," Rajah said at the bench. "Don't let that empty net fool you. If you get a chance — skate out with it. Once you're over centre, you can shoot all you want. No icing. We don't want to create a faceoff in our end. Right?"

"Right!" we all shouted.

On that last shift I won the draw, and got the puck back to Simon. He skated around our net and shot it off the boards by our blue line, just as Rajah had taught us.

The Cougars' defence couldn't keep it in, and they took the puck at centre ice. I skated out, rushed the defenceman who was coming in and poked the puck off his stick. I reached behind me to get it and skated hard toward the Cougars' goal.

I knew I had to get to centre.

One stride over centre I leaned on my stick to get a wrist shot away. The empty net looked small even from that distance.

But before I could shoot, someone lifted my stick and the chance — and with it the puck — was gone.

I turned to see Reisberry rushing to our blue line with a full head of steam. He bounced the puck once off the boards to get around Willie, cut inside neatly as Simon came to meet him, and moved straight in at Vickie in goal.

Again, Vickie didn't fall for his fake.

She followed him across as he faded to his left. To do so, she had to sweep off her feet and keep both pads up to block his chance.

This time Reisberry kept his cool. He pivoted, glided backward, and when Vickie had completed the slide across the goal mouth, he lifted the puck cleanly over her stacked pads.

1–1.

We were headed for overtime again.

# 16

# Deflection!

From the drop of the puck it was like another game. The Cougars were charged, too, but I got the impression they were holding something back. Maybe they were afraid of getting caught again.

From the bench, I looked out at Vickie. If there is one player who feels the pressure in sudden-death overtime, it has to be the goalie. It doesn't matter how well you play — make that one mistake that lets in the winning goal, and it's over. You can never shake the feeling that the loss is all your fault. I was glad that Vickie was in goal, not me.

In the stands, Vickie's mother and my mother stood side by side.

From the first shift, the Cougars' game plan was clear. They were playing strong, defensive hockey, with two defence well back, and two forwards in the centre ice area. They watched for us to make a mistake. If they got a chance, one player would start a solo rush. The rest of their team would hang back to make sure we didn't get a return rush.

The thing was, they had enough fast players that they could do that and still be a real threat.

Two of them did break in early on, but Vickie stoned them cold with her stand-up style.

We got several chances, too. From the point again, Willie let three or four slappers go. Two went by the far corner about knee-high, but the other two were so wild they ended up in downtown Newtonville bouncing off lampposts.

Morley hit the post.

Every shift we were up against Lars and Reisberry. Their coach was forcing that match-up. I now had to admit they were both faster than me. It kind of amazed me that Jenny Lau, on my left wing, was able to keep up with Reisberry. All I could do with Lars was to try to get in his way. If he got a good start and had any room, that was not easy.

What Rajah had not told us was that the overtime period, at fifteen minutes, was "stop time." All season we had played without stopping the clock. In the playoffs, however, we played the last two minutes of each period as stop time, where the time clock stops every time the play stops, just like the pros.

But a whole period of stop time?

Rajah had us on shorter shifts, changing on the go. Even still, by the time the first overtime was winding down, we had all begun to feel tired. My legs wouldn't move fast enough.

When the buzzer sounded, we were bushed. We were also in deeper trouble. The rules also said that after a period of overtime, we would continue into a second period. But with every minute of play now, we dropped one player. That meant there was more room on the ice — and more chance that the Cougars, with their speed, would dominate.

After the first full period of overtime, each team dropped one player. That made it four on four. Nerve-racking.

Five minutes of that, and then we'd go to three on three; after another five minutes, two on two. If the game lasted long enough we'd be down to one on one, with the goalies.

Nobody wanted that.

Once we went to four on four, the Cougars didn't give us much of a chance. Once, when Rajah managed to escape the Cougars' match-up, I watched from the bench as Lars and Reisberry circled in our end like vultures after roadkill. One of their defence players hit the goalposts — twice, one on each side. The game looked more like a power play than four on four.

When the buzzer sounded, Rajah signalled Jenny and me to go out, along with Willie. Three on three.

"Two forwards?" I asked.

"You've also played defence, Jake. So do it." Rajah patted the top of my helmet and I skated out. "You're the only guy we've got with rep hockey speed. We need you out there to match those guys."

I was staring at Rajah, but he was now focused on other players. A few feet out on the ice I looked back at our bench. *Our* bench. I realized for the first time, *really* realized, that we were now a team with one purpose. Whatever happened, it would be *this* team that did it. Good or bad.

The faceoff was just outside our blue line. I won the draw, but Reisberry moved up and intercepted my pass back to Willie on defence.

Reisberry cut in fast, leaving Willie standing flat-footed. Vickie came out of the net high, cutting the angle. Reisberry read this. Halfway through the circle he cut sharply toward the centre to get by her and have an open net to shoot at.

By then Willie had recovered and he re-appeared as though out of nowhere. He cut sharply right, just over the blue line. He didn't line Reisberry up or anything. He just skated hard. Reisberry was moving fast. He had his head down and his stick cocked for a slapshot.

When he did look up and saw Willie, he tried to pull one shoulder in and turn sideways. Willie caught him in the right shoulder. You could hear the thud throughout the rink. Just: *thunk*! No echo. Reisberry spun four times before he hit the ice.

He didn't bounce.

Willie picked up the loose puck and stickhandled it back to centre, methodically, and just when he had drawn their centre player out to check him, he dumped the puck into the Cougars' zone.

Jenny used her speed to beat everybody to the puck in the corner. I headed for behind the net and picked up her quick pass.

My wrap-around almost worked, but the Cougars' goalie jammed his skate against the post. The puck came free again. I cycled it back behind the net to Jenny, who drew two Cougars out of position before feeding Willie a pass out by the blue line.

Willie wound up and blasted one.

I skated out to the corner of the crease again. Willie's shot missed. I held my stick up so the blade caught the shot just below my knee. The puck flipped up, still missed the net and made a clunking sound as it hit the glass.

I grabbed the puck behind the net. I ragged it back and forth, shifting my weight to fake coming out one side and then the other. Reisberry was slow getting back to check me. The Cougars' goalie slid back and forth, trying to turn his head to see what I was doing. If he turned one way, I moved the other way.

Meanwhile, Jenny headed for the front of the goal. Or at least, she tried to. The Cougars kept her covered well, keeping between me and both her and Willie.

There was one thing I knew they couldn't do — send somebody back behind the net to get me. As soon as they did, I would skate out the other way. That would put three of us — me, Willie and Jenny — in front of the net. At the same time, they would have only two players to defend, since their third forward would still be behind the goal trying to find me.

So I dipsy-doodled behind the net, while Willie and Jenny looked for openings that weren't there.

Then I sighted Willie coming across. I came out on the goalie's left-hand side. Fearing a wraparound, he jammed his skates and pads tight to the post. Instead, I threw a pass at the far circle, at the only clear patch of ice.

Willie picked up the pass. Still in mid-stride, he cocked his stick back and let the slapshot go.

For a nanosecond, the arena was still. Everything turned to slow motion: Willie raising his stick; the goalie moving to his right to meet the shot; Jenny twisting away from her check; my strides as I tried to plant myself at the edge of the crease.

I've told you about Willie's slapshot. Maybe a million times.

This time, he got everything on it.

It came in like a freight train — on wobbly tracks.

In my slow-motion molasses world I could see it all the way in. And though the arena was packed and rattled with fans, what I could hear was the music of Grandpa Gord's fiddle.

"Ta-teedle-deedle-deedle da-da teedle-deedle-da, ta teedle-deedle …"

But this time it was Willie who was playing the tune, setting the time.

Kaw-zunk! Zip! Ting!

The shot came in knee-high, but it would have missed the net. From the edge of the crease I caught it perfectly on the lower shaft of my stick, deflecting it with a bunting motion into the empty side of the net.

Kaw-zunk! Zip! Ting!

Score!

# 17

## Celebration

The arena burst into a cheering and slapping of sticks and cowbells and bugles. The Bear Claws collapsed in a heap at centre ice. From the bottom of the pile I didn't get to see much of that.

Finally, we all kind of shook ourselves loose, and congratulated each other, and then lined up for the usual handshake.

First in line for the Cougars was Lars Allrick. Up close with his helmet off, you could see a small scar on his lower lip.

"Great game," he said, slapping hands with me.

I gripped his hand. "Sorry about the stick thing," I said. "It was an accident."

Lars smiled at me. "But that last goal was no accident," he said. "That was a great deflection. I didn't think anybody could see Willie's slapshots." He gave me a mild tap with the back of his hand and moved on down the line.

Last in line was Jamie Reisberry.

He touched hands as though I had some bad disease. Then he stopped, turned.

"Henry," he said.

I didn't know if he was going to pile into me or what.

"Nice goal," he said, finally. He paused. "You playing rep next year?"

I didn't know what to say.

"You should," Reisberry said. "You're good, Jake. Could be tougher, but you're good."

I looked at him strangely. He grinned. "And sorry about that cross-check. Sometimes I get steamed up." He gave me a light tap on the shoulder.

"No problem, Jamie," I said.

The Bear Claws celebrated with a feast of wings in a sports pub. Parents and friends joined us. It was as noisy there as the arena.

Tyler stood on his chair. "Here's to Grandpa Cowbells," he said. "Our noisiest fan!"

Grandpa Ron told everybody — and I mean everybody — about going to school with Bobby Hull. Some fathers even remembered Hull when he played.

"Here's to all grandfathers," said Jenny Lau. "Everywhere."

Grandpa P.J. kept shaking Coach Rajah's hand, and telling everybody who would listen (and many who wouldn't): "Did you know this guy played for Canada in the World Juniors one year? He has a gold ring! Where do they get coaches like this?"

"And he has taken umpteen coaching courses," said Grandpa Ron. "Not like in the old days."

"And you, Jacob Henry," said my mother. "Nanny Joyce and I have a bone to pick with you."

"What do you mean?" I asked.

"The quilt rack in the basement," said Nanny Joyce. "Something's happened to it."

"Oh-oh," I said, afraid of what was coming.

"Just because it looks like a hockey goal doesn't mean you get to use it for one," said my mother. "No more, you hear?" She said it with a wide smile but I knew she still meant it.

"I had to practice deflections somewhere," I said.

In one corner, my dad and Fred had set up a chess board and had begun a game.

"You two don't forget there's a celebration going on here," said my mother. The chess players both waved her away.

Grandpa Gord squeezed his way between tables to the little stage in the corner. He set up Nanny Joyce's keyboard and took out his fiddle.

"Oh no!" I said. "Not now!"

But as soon as Nanny Joyce started playing, and Grandpa Gord put the fiddle to his chin, the team started cheering and clapping.

"Yee-haw," yelled Coach Rajah, slapping his cap on his thigh.

The fiddle music bounced off the walls and rattled the dishes. Vickie got up and did a step dance. I didn't even know she took lessons.

I could not have thought of a better way to celebrate our victory.

# Other books you'll enjoy in the Sports Stories series

## Baseball

❏ *Curve Ball* by John Danakas #1
Tom Poulos is looking forward to a summer of baseball in Toronto until his mother puts him on a plane to Winnipeg.

❏ *Baseball Crazy* by Martyn Godfrey #10
Rob Carter wins an all-expenses-paid chance to be bat boy at the Blue Jays spring training camp in Florida.

❏ *Shark Attack* by Judi Peers #25
The East City Sharks have a good chance of winning the county championship until their arch rivals get a tough new pitcher.

❏ *Hit and Run* by Dawn Hunter and Karen Hunter #35
Glen Thomson is a talented pitcher, but as his ego inflates, team morale plummets. Will he learn from being benched for losing his temper?

❏ *Power Hitter* by C. A. Forsyth #41
Connor's summer was looking like a write-off. That is, until he discovered his secret talent.

❏ *Sayonara, Sharks* by Judi Peers #48
In this sequel to *Shark Attact*, Ben and Kate are excited about the school trip to Japan, but Matt's not sure he wants to go.

❏ *Out of Bounds* by Sylvia Gunnery # 70
When the Hirtle family's house burns down, Jay is forced to relocate and switch schools. He has a choice: sacrifice a year of basketball or play on the same team as his arch-rival Mike.

## Basketball

❏ *Fast Break* by Michael Coldwell #8
Moving from Toronto to small-town Nova Scotia was rough, but when Jeff makes the school basketball team he thinks things are looking up.

# Ice Hockey

❏ *Two Minutes for Roughing* by Joseph Romain #2
As a new player on a tough Toronto hockey team, Les must fight to fit in.

❏ *Hockey Night in Transcona* by John Danakas #7
Cody Powell gets promoted to the Transcona Sharks' first line, bumping out the coach's son, who's not happy with the change.

❏ *Face Off* by C. A. Forsyth #13
A talented hockey player finds himself competing with his best friend for a spot on a select team.

❏ *Hat Trick* by Jacqueline Guest #20
The only girl on an all-boy hockey team works to earn the captain's respect and her mother's approval.

❏ *Hockey Heroes* by John Danakas #22
A left-winger on the thirteen-year-old Transcona Sharks adjusts to a new best friend and his mom's boyfriend.

❏ *Hockey Heat Wave* by C. A. Forsyth #27
In this sequel to *Face Off*, Zack and Mitch run into trouble when it looks as if only one of them will make the select team at hockey camp.

❏ *Shoot to Score* by Sandra Richmond #31
Playing defense on the B list alongside the coach's mean-spirited son is a tough obstacle for Steven to overcome, but he perseveres and changes his luck.

❏ *Rookie Season* by Jacqueline Guest #42
What happens when a boy wants to join an all-girl hockey team?

❏ *Brothers on Ice* by John Danakas #44
Brothers Dylan and Deke both want to play goal for the same team.

❏ *Rink Rivals* by Jacqueline Guest #49
A move to Calgary finds the Evans twins pitted against each other on the ice, and struggling to help each other out of trouble.

❏ *Power Play* by Michele Martin Bossley #50
An early-season injury causes Zach Thomas to play timidly, and a school bully just makes matters worse. Will a famous hockey player be able to help Zach sort things out?

❏ *Danger Zone* by Michele Martin Bossley #56
When Jason accidentally checks a player from behind, the boy is seriously hurt. Jason is devastated when the boy's parents want him suspended from the league.

❏ *Ice Attack* by Beatrice Vandervelde #58
Alex and Bill used to be an unbeatable combination on the Lakers hockey team. Now that they are enemies, Alex is thinking about quitting.

❏ *Red-Line Blues* by Camilla Reghelini Rivers #59
Lee's hockey coach is only interested in the hotshots on his team. Ordinary players like him spend their time warming the bench.

❏ *Goon Squad* by Michele Martin Bossley #63
Jason knows he shouldn't play dirty, but the coach of his hockey team is telling him otherwise. This book is the exciting follow-up to *Power Play* and *Danger Zone*.

❏ *Ice Dreams* by Beverly Scudamore #65
Twelve-year-old Maya is a talented figure skater, just as her mother was before she died four years ago. Despite pressure from her family to keep skating, Maya tries to pursue her passion for goaltending.

❏ *Interference* by Lorna Schultz Nicholson #68
Josh has finally made it to an elite hockey team, but his undiagnosed type one diabetes is working against him — and getting more serious by the day.

❏ *Deflection* by Bill Swan #71
Justin and his two best friends play road hockey together and are members of the same league team. But some personal rivalries and interference from Justin's three all-too-supportive grandfathers start to create tension among the players.

❏ *Misconduct* by Beverly Scudamore #72
Matthew has always been a popular student and hockey player. But after an altercation with a tough kid named Dillon at hockey camp, Matt finds himself number one on the bully's hit list.

❏ *Roughing* by Lorna Schultz Nicholson #74
Josh has finally made it to an elite hockey team but no one knows that he has Type 1 diabetes — and it's getting more serious by the day.

❏ *Home Ice* by Beatrice Vandervelde #76
Tori is staying with family near Toronto while her parents deal with troubles back home. To keep a sense of normalcy, she joins the Rangers — the worst hockey team in the league.

## Roller Hockey

❏ *Roller Hockey Blues* by Steven Barwin and Gabriel David Tick #17
Mason Ashbury faces a summer of boredom until he makes the roller hockey team.

## Running

❏ *Fast Finish* by Bill Swan #30
Noah is a promising young runner headed for the provincial finals when he suddenly decides to withdraw from the event.

## Sailing

❏ *Sink or Swim* by William Pasnak #5
Dario can barely manage the dog paddle, but thanks to his mother he's spending the summer at a water sports camp.

## Soccer

❏ *Lizzie's Soccer Showdown* by John Danakas #3
When Lizzie asks why the boys and girls can't play together, she finds herself the new captain of the soccer team.

❏ *Alecia's Challenge* by Sandra Diersch #32
Thirteen-year-old Alecia has to cope with a new school, a new step-father, and friends who have suddenly discovered the opposite sex.

❏ *Shut-Out!* by Camilla Reghelini Rivers #39
David wants to play soccer more than anything, but will the new coach let him?

❏ *Offside!* by Sandra Diersch #43
Alecia has to confront a new girl who drives her teammates crazy.

❏ *Heads Up!* by Dawn Hunter and Karen Hunter #45
Do the Warriors really need a new, hot-shot player who skips practice?

❏ *Off the Wall* by Camilla Reghelini Rivers #52
Lizzie loves indoor soccer, and she's thrilled when her little sister gets into the sport. But when their teams are pitted against each other, Lizzie can only warn her sister to watch out.

❏ *Trapped!* by Michele Martin Bossley #53
There's a thief on Jane's soccer team, and everyone thinks it's her best friend, Ashley. Jane must find the true culprit to save both Ashley and the team's morale.

❏ *Soccer Star!* by Jacqueline Guest #61
Samantha longs to show up Carly, the school's reigning soccer star, but her new interest in theatre is taking up a lot of her time. Can she really do it all?

❏ *Miss Little's Losers* by Robert Rayner #64
The Brunswick Valley School soccer team haven't won a game all season long. When their coach resigns, the only person who will coach them is Miss Little … their former kindergarten teacher!

❏ *Corner Kick* by Bill Swan #66
A fierce rivalry erupts between Michael Strike, captain of both the school soccer and chess teams, and Zahir, a talented newcomer from the Middle East.

❏ *Just for Kicks* by Robert Rayner #69
When their parents begin taking their games too seriously, it's up to the soccer-mad gang from Brunswick Valley School to reclaim the spirit of their sport.

❏ *Play On* by Sandra Diersch #73

Alecia's soccer team is preparing for the championship game but their game is suffering as the players get distracted by other interests. Can they renew their commitment to their sport in order to make it to the finals?

❏ *Suspended* by Robert Rayner #75

Shay and his pal Toby are among the players on the school soccer team who fall foul of the "fair play contract". The players form their own unofficial team — and become one of the league's top teams. But will they be allowed to play in the championship game?

## Track and Field

❏ *Mikayla's Victory* by Cynthia Bates #29

Mikayla must compete against her friend if she wants to represent her school at an important track event.

❏ *Walker's Runners* by Robert Rayner #55

Toby Morton hates gym. In fact, he doesn't run for anything — except the classroom door. Then Mr. Walker arrives and persuades Toby to join the running team.

❏ *Mud Run* by Bill Swan #60

No one in the S.T. Lovey Cross-Country Club is running with the pack, until the new coach demonstrates the value of teamwork.

❏ *Off Track* by Bill Swan #62

Twelve-year-old Tyler is stuck in summer school and banned from watching TV and playing computer games. His only diversion is training for a triathlon race … except when it comes to the swimming requirement.